AF480773

*A person finds joy in giving an apt reply—
and how good is a timely word!*

Proverbs 15:23

Foreword

Naga society is a society in fast paced transition. The society has transformed so rapidly that a young aspirant who is facing an interview finds difficulty connecting the dots on issues facing Naga society.

Often, the aspirant living through the current reality finds the things he hears from his parents or the things he reads quite removed from his lived experience. The interviewer asks questions from his vantage point which the interviewee fails to make sense. The book is a modest attempt to make sense of such questions. I have drawn extensively from own interactions with people throughout my sad 34 years. No great work of scholarship is claimed.

 I do owe a depth of intellectual gratitude to Prof Francis Fukuyama, Dr Jelle JP Wouters and Laxmikant.

To make the best use of the book, frame answers in your own words the questions that exist at the beginning of each chapter, read the chapter and the model answers. The book simply seeks to initiate a discussion with the reader.

Chothazo Nienu

Preface

This book, Contemporary Issues in Nagaland Explained, is written for young aspirants appearing for interviews in competitive examinations in Nagaland. Over the years, I have had the privilege of engaging with many such aspirants who reach out to me for guidance. These conversations revealed a gap between academic literature and the books typically consulted for exam preparation. Academic works tend to be narrow in scope due to methodological constraints, while preparatory books largely focus on factual recall. Newspaper opinion pieces can help to some extent but often devolve into complaints rather than structured explanations.

This book attempts to bridge that gap. It is written in accessible language and aims to explain the contemporary issues confronting Naga society by combining analytical rigour with contextual understanding.

The Intellectual Journey

Both as a student and a teacher of economics, I have been interested in understanding a framework that successfully explains the issues confronting Naga society, especially the economic problems. My first search was in the economics discipline. However, economics as a discipline has several limitations in explaining issues facing Naga society. Consider this: Mainstream economic theory rests on three fundamental assumptions:

1. Rationality — the belief that people prefer more to less, now to later, and that they operate with perfect information.
2. Self-interest — the idea that individual gain leads to collective efficiency, famously captured by Adam Smith's "invisible hand."
3. Atomistic individual — the notion that society is composed solely of individuals or firms acting independently

These assumptions, while useful for theoretical clarity, are overly simplistic, downplaying factors such as social norms, power structures, historical context, cultural influences, institutions and the bounded rationality of real human behavior — all of which significantly shape economic outcomes in the real world. These limitations have resulted in the development of alternative schools of thought. Of the different schools of thought, I found Institutional Economics most applicable to Nagaland.

Institutional Economics holds that economic performance depends on the strength of institutions — especially property rights and contract enforcement – tasks society performs (informal institutions) with the state playing an important role (formal institutions).

In Nagaland, however, the presence of strong tribal affiliations and underground groups (more politely, Naga political groups) that prohibits private transactions and extort money from businesses undermines private property rights. According to this school, such practices harm long-term economic outcomes.

But the framework fell short in answering a deeper question: Why are government institutions in Nagaland unable to protect property rights in the first place? Institutional Economics attributes the failure to weak incentives — the idea that people in power do not have enough motivation to uphold the rule of law. But this is not a complete explanation. Why do they lack the incentive? Because they either lack authority, or the people do not recognize that authority. A government that lacks authority, or a situation where people do not recognize governmental authority, falls outside the scope of economics and is more relevant to political science and sociology.

While reading the works of Jelle J.P. Wouters, an anthropologist who has worked closely in Nagaland, I found many of his insights compelling. However, I also felt that anthropology's guiding principle of cultural relativism – its reluctance to pass judgment on cultural practices – often limited its ability to confront certain dysfunctions within Naga society head-on. It was after reading political scientist Francis Fukuyama and author Fareed Zakaria, that I found in their works a political lens through which many of Nagaland's institutional problems began to make sense.

The core insight I derived is this: Nagaland's enduring dysfunctions are largely the result of a weak and fragmented state structure.

The Nature of a Weak State

Several historical and structural factors have contributed to the weakness of the state in Nagaland:

1. Late introduction to modern state institutions
2. The long-standing Naga political struggle for self-determination
3. Rising literacy, economic capacity, and connectivity enabling strong tribal and village-based mobilization, often in competition with state authority

A state is often defined, following Max Weber, as "a human community that (successfully) claims the monopoly of the legitimate use of physical force within a given territory." In India's constitutional framework (Article 12), the state includes legislative and executive bodies at all levels — central, state, and local.

The traditional Naga society was built around village autonomy and communitarianism, with no centralised bureaucratic apparatus. Our identities are deeply rooted in our villages, not in a unified polity. Thus, modern state structures — with their hierarchy, impersonality, and legal-rational authority — were seen as foreign impositions.

Nagaland's statehood was perceived as illegitimate. Those who negotiated the terms of statehood were branded traitors; some were assassinated. The state was seen not as an expression of democratic will but as a bastard institution, born of compromise and lacking moral legitimacy. While the central government helped institutionalise democratic forms, it often avoided asserting its authority, especially in the face of widespread corruption, for fear of exacerbating secessionist sentiment. This avoidance has contributed to the creation of a weak state: the government's authority being fragile and unable to enforce accountability.

Reinforcing the State

In the six decades since statehood, public trust in state institutions has slowly grown. However, strengthening state capacity will depend on two key changes:
1. Better use of central funds — Nagaland has some of the lowest tax rates in the country for fuel and vehicle registration. However, any discussion on increasing state revenue is met with

opposition, largely due to the poor utilisation of public funds. 2. Ending extortion by political groups — The nearly 30 Naga political groups extract "taxes" from citizens and businesses, further weakening the formal state and harming economic activity.

Nagas today are more organised than ever. However, the nature of these organisations is often contradictory. As sociologist Ferdinand Tönnies noted, Gemeinschaft (community) is rooted in emotional bonds, while Gesellschaft (civil society) is characterised by formality and impersonal structures. Many Naga organisations present themselves as Gemeinschaft but function more like Gesellschaft.

Identity-based groups in Nagaland often assume functions that should belong to the state — such as dispute resolution, protection from political groups, and fight for allocation of government resources for its members. The government, in the public's imagination, is seen merely as a provider of resources. Pride is associated with the existence of government institutions in one's community. This has led to a scenario where communities aggressively lobby for state institutions (e.g., administrative offices) not on merit but through political manoeuvring.

Nagaland: The California of India?

The broadly three pillars of power in the state: the state government, the tribal apex bodies and Naga political groups often operate at cross-purposes, weakening constitutional governance.

In terms of governmental weakness, Nagaland resembles California — a progressive state with strong civil society but paralyzed by overregulation and litigation. Host of CNN podcast

Global Public Square, Fareed Zakaria, noted in the context of governmental authority, "To distribute power, you first need power." Nagaland's civil society is so strong and the state so weak that even a well-organized clan can effectively challenge the authority of the state.

Communitisation: A Response to State Failure

One reform attempted in Nagaland is Communitisation — an institutional arrangement in which village communities take over management of public services. Legally established in 2002, it was rolled out in electricity, education, and health.

Initially, Communitisation worked well, especially when backed by central schemes like Sarva Shiksha Abhiyan and financial aid from the central government. However, enthusiasm waned once funds dried up. Bureaucrats also found community oversight burdensome.

While Communitisation improved health services somewhat, it failed to address systemic issues like staff shortages and bureaucratic friction. In education and power, its effectiveness has either plateaued or declined.

Celebrating Nagaland

Rather than viewing the state as a betrayal of Naga cause for self-determination, it is worthwhile to treat it as an achievement that requires strengthening.

India's political consensus remains firm on three issues:

- No compromise on territorial integrity
- Development of nuclear capability for nuclear deterrence

- Continuation of affirmative action in the form of reservations

The Naga struggle for self-determination directly conflicts with the first since redrawing India's borders is a non-starter. The best viable path forward for the Nagas is to develop and strengthen the state of Nagaland.

Chothazo Nienu

Table of Contents

Abbreviations Used in the Book

AAP	Aam Aadmi Party
AFSPA	Armed Forces (Special Powers) Act (AFSPA), 1958
CNTC	Central Nagaland Tribes Council
DGP	Director General of Police
ENPO	Eastern Nagaland People's Organization
ENSF	Eastern Nagaland Students' Federation
FIR	First Information Report
FMR	Free Movement Regime
GPF	General Provident Fund
GSDP	Gross State Domestic Product
GST	Goods and Services Tax
HQ	Head Quarter
ILP	Inner Line Permit
MLA	Member of Legislative Assembly
NBCC	Nagaland Baptist Church Council
NLTP	Nagaland Liquor Prohibition Act (NLTP Act), 1989
NMOOP	National Mission on Oil Seeds and Oil Palm
NNC	Naga Nationalist Council
NPA	Non-Performing Asset
NSCN -IM	National Socialist Council of Nagaland (Isak-Muivah)

PIMS	Personal Information Management System
PPP	Public-Private Partnership
PWID	People Who Inject Drugs
RTE	Right to Education
SMC	School Management Committee
USA	United States of America
VDB	Village Development Board
VEC	Village Education Committee
VC	Village Council

1

Contemporary Nagaland through the eyes of three generations

GOVERNANCE FAILURE AND SOCIETAL CONTRADICTIONS: UNDERSTANDING WHY NAGALAND IS THE WAY IT IS

The story is apocryphal at best, but the story is told of a person belonging to the Konyak tribe who in the 1970s was part of a Naga delegation to meet the former Prime Minister of India, Smt Indira Gandhi, at Kolkatta to discuss the Indo-Naga political issue. Meeting such a high dignitary, the man travelled the short distance in Kolkatta by helicopter to meet the former Prime Minister, and having met her, travelled back to Dimapur from Kolkatta by train, travelled to Mon (his district HQ) by bus and walked the rest of his journey to his village. In a period lasting barely a week, the man experienced several realities: the most advanced form of travel - air - as also the most mundane - walking.

When one looks at Nagaland in its totality, one is still confronted with similar reality the Konyak encountered 50 years back.

Similar to how the Konyak faced several realities within the span of a week, a Naga faces multiple realities in his daily life. A Naga is confronted with the might of the Indian state through the AFSPA on the one hand and the complete lawlessness on the other at a place like the Dimapur-Assam border where all goods entering Nagaland are faced with extortion. The NSCN-IM and other Naga political groups celebrate Naga Independence Day on 14 August every year; the Chief Minister hoists the Indian tricolour the next day. In the Nagaland Legislative Assembly, the highest decision-making body in Nagaland under the Indian Constitution, members declare that democratic voting is alien to the Nagas and Nagas should revert to consensus decision making! A clan threatens the Government of Nagaland that it would not be held responsible for the course of actions that it takes. One can cite many more contradictions.

To a young Naga, the contradictions are perceived not as inconsistencies but as failures of the state. The young Naga sees these contradictions as reflections of the state's inability to address critical issues effectively. This leads to a sense of disillusionment and frustration with the governance and political system.

The state's consistent failure has been confirmed repeatedly through the low SDG scores published by the NITI Aayog.

To a Naga elder, the views are often very different. Talk to an elder and he will narrate the difficulties of the previous generation and how things have improved. "Things are easier now: we receive piped water; during our time, women folks had to rise early in the morning to go carry water. Rice mill came while we were young, before that we had to help our mothers pound the flour. We consumed meat only during festivals or when someone hunted successfully; now, we can have meat anytime we want. Rice was a luxury, we had *galho* every night to conserve rice. People had to study using kerosene lamps, now you can study as and when you want. The Indian army burnt the village granary and we had to starve that year!"

Essential Insights 1.1: Key Governance Failures and Developmental Gaps in Nagaland

1. Nepotism in awarding government contracts
2. Shoddy execution of government projects
3. Embezzlement of funds through cuts by various stakeholders, from political parties to institutional heads and underground groups
4. Poor road conditions and lack of repairs
5. Backdoor appointments or recruitment into government services without fair competitive exams
6. Inconsistent water supply
7. Non-functioning government schools, particularly in rural areas
8. Ineffective waste-collection and treatment systems
9. Law and order issues where the community is the primary responder
10. Over-dependence on the central government and lack of state revenue generation

Which of the two views is correct? In reality, both are valid. Naga contact with modern political institutions was very recent. Added to this, the popular support for the Naga political movement made the modern institutions represented by the Government of India and Government of Nagaland appear illegitimate. Whether it was the Government of India or the Government of Nagaland, the state (represented by the two) could not assert its power effectively. At the same time, the Government of India through generous endowments developed physical and non-physical infrastructure in the state without proper audit on how these resources were spent. This lack of oversight coupled with lack of acceptance of the state government's authority became a breeding ground for corruption.

For a Naga elder, the state's development has been quite rapid, it has become unrecognisable. For a Naga youth, the economic, social and political reality can be exasperating.

Contemporary Nagaland: Through the Eyes of Three Generations

From the point of view of their experience with modern political institutions, contemporary [1] Nagaland can be viewed through the eyes of three different generations[2]:

1.   **The tail-end of the village republic:** This generation lived approximately a hundred years ago and had experience of morungs, deep jungles, tales of headhunting from their parents, and contacts with the British.

2.   **The generation that saw the independence of India, the birth of Nagaland and Naga freedom movement**

3.   **The present generation (starting the 1980s and 1990s)**

The first generation mentioned here experienced statelessness or at best a state whose commitment to the welfare of the people was minimal either because of incapability or because its interest was elsewhere. The second generation experienced the initial functioning of a modern state characterised by its bureaucratic hierarchies and specialised functions along with a state called

---

[1] Contemporary here is used in the same sense one uses 'contemporary history of India' for a history of India from independence till today. Contemporary here is thus not a snapshot of the present but a period lasting roughly a 100 years. Some Naga tribes, like the Aos and the Angamis have had earlier contact with modern institutions compared to other tribes.

[2] The term 'generation' here is being used loosely. The idea is not to give an exact definition but to highlight how different generations experience with modern state institutions evolved.

Nagaland which they thought was temporary or was viewed as illegitimate. The present generation accepts the legitimacy of the state, knows its functions and duties, and comment angrily on social media about its failures!

Community as the principal feature of Naga Tribal Society: Through the eyes of the first generation with vestigial remains in the second generation

The community played a significant role in the way people lived. The community here has three layers: the clan, the village and the tribe. The primary community through which a Naga viewed himself however was the village community.

The average Naga had very little contact outside of his village. These villages were walled, and heavily protected. This led to isolation,[3] also leading to the development of many dialects.

---

[3] A nuanced reading of isolation in village republics is required. While an ordinary Naga was mostly cocooned in his village, there were people within the village who went on head-hunting expeditions, engaged in trade with tephremia in the plains to buy metal, salt and ornaments, and had trade relations with nearby villages and tribes. Naga individuals or different groups also migrated to plant new villages or were forced to migrate to new villages when they were excommunicated. These were however minimal. In fact, at times, because of inter-clan rivalry or hostilities which could be non-consequential but nevertheless disruptive a person might be hesitant to venture beyond his immediate neighbourhood. Different clans could also cultivate different regions limiting contact with other clans' members except during times of festivals (a common retort even now is "Since we don't belong to that part of the village, we have not been able to know you"). Even inter-clan within a village, variation of certain words in their dialects were thus noticed.

Activities beyond one's villages, however, was proof that Nagas were not savages killing anyone on a whim. Dr Venusa Tinyi, in his paper 'The Headhunting Culture of the Nagas: Reinterpreting the Self' discusses the linguistic and cultural distinction between two terms used in the Chokri language of the Chakhesang Nagas: *ga* and *dothri* - both terms means killing. However, the term ga is a neutral descriptor for killing, applied in contexts like

Villages also had their own territories. Each individual or family owned their own plots of land. No Naga was landless since land was found in plenty relative to the existing population. Villages also had defined territories and shared their boundaries with other villages. The concept of conquering over another village and colonising them or collecting tax from them did not exist or at best was minimal and inconsequential to a large extent.

A village was thus self-contained and self-sufficient. In modern usage, villages have been labelled "village republics". All these gave rise to people locating their identity primarily to their village.

People would go to fields together to work, which they did so for companionship as also for security. They worked in each other's fields. Working in each other's fields was a way of exchanging labour. '*Mele krothos*' in Chokri Chakhesang dialect or '*peli krotho*' in Tenyidie were formed where young people would come together to work alternately in each person's fields. They socialise in such settings. Socialisations occurred at night also in morungs where songs, poems, and stories were shared with values, morals and socially acceptable behaviour passed down in such gatherings.

---

hunting *(thi-ga)* or wartime killings *(mi-ga)*, without any moral implication. In contrast, *dothri* signifies killing with moral judgment, often associated with murder.

Venusa Tinyi, "The Headhunting Culture of the Nagas: Reinterpreting the Self," The South Asianist Journal 5, no. 1 (Spring 2017): Special Section - Nagas in the 21st Century, published May 6, 2017.

Festivals were celebrated together. There were festivals where going to field to work on those occasions was taboo. Festivals were occasions to gather, sing songs, play games, eat and drink.

Building house, pulling stones, celebrating feast of merit, all these were done together by the community. In building one's house, the common practice was for the person building the house to gather the material such as straw, wood, and bamboo. For the actual construction however, neighbours and clan members would gather to construct the house.

People came together to each other's help during times of emergencies such as sickness and death. To look the other way when a member of the community was in trouble would invite gossip and censure.

Honesty and hard-work stem partly from this close-knit community as they were valued and celebrated. Both dishonesty and laziness invite gossip and censure.

Consensus and consensus-building was a natural corollary of community bond, where honour, honesty and sacrifice were valued. Every male[4] present, regardless of his social standing, was given opportunity to express his opinions following which decisions were arrived at. Voting as a system of taking decision was absent.

Superstitious beliefs and religion were strengthened by the community. There were superstitious beliefs which absolutely forbid certain actions which were enforced through the community.

Justice was community-based. Often an action against an individual was interpreted as an action against the whole community. Revenge could be taken against any member from that community.

---

[4] In recent years, the exclusion of women in public sphere in Naga traditional decision making has been well highlighted.

It was this Naga society the British came in contact with. The British did introduce several modern institutions to the Nagas. However, these were peripheral rather than transformative, as they failed to penetrate deeply into the traditional structures and social fabric of Naga society. The institutions, such as the establishment of colonial administration, rudimentary education systems, and limited economic infrastructure, were often implemented to serve the administrative and political interests of the British rather than to foster substantial societal change.

For example, while the British set up administrative frameworks, these were largely limited to controlling conflicts, collecting taxes, or ensuring order in specific areas of strategic importance. They did not significantly alter or replace the Naga village system, which remained self-governing and autonomous in many aspects. Similarly, education introduced during this time reached only a small section of the population, mostly in areas closer to British administrative centers, and its content was often tailored to produce individuals who could serve the colonial system rather than empower the broader population.

Economically, the British focus was on resource extraction and ensuring trade routes, rather than developing a self-sustaining local economy. As a result, the traditional subsistence-based economy of the Nagas remained largely unchanged.

In essence, while the British institutions left a footprint, their impact was limited to the margins of Naga society, failing to deeply integrate or reshape its core social, cultural, and political structures.

The full process of political development talk about in political science literature did not take place in Nagaland. This explains many contradictions one sees today.

Contemporary Nagaland through the eyes of the Second Generation

Nagaland was created in 1963. The state emerged through fraught political violence. The idea of an independent Nagalim is a distant reality now but Nagas who initially fought for it truly believed in their cause. And who could blame them! To many Nagas, mainland Indians were and are still considered foreigners. Analysing the words Nagas used to describe members from other tribes and mainland Indians reveal this attitude. The words *tephremia* in Tenyidie and *tsumar* in Ao are designated for mainland Indians, both terms mean "foreigner" or "alien". In Chokri Chakhesang dialect, *"so rünami"* means "guests from other villages" which would apply to every Naga when used more generously while *"so tephremi"* means "guests from

Essential Insights 1.2 Theory of Political Development: From band-level society to the state

A theory of political development posits that political organization evolves from simple, band-level societies to complex state structures through a series of progressive stages. Initially, band-level societies operate on informal, kin-based relationships with minimal centralized authority. As societies grow and become more complex, they transition to tribal or chiefdom structures, where leadership becomes more formalized and hierarchical. Eventually, these societies develop into state-level systems, characterized by centralized governance, codified laws, and institutionalized bureaucracy. This evolution reflects increasing social complexity, economic development, and the need for more sophisticated mechanisms to manage larger populations and more diverse interests.

Family: The basic unit of social organization, comprising individuals related by blood or marriage.

Band: A small group of families or kinship units that live together and cooperate for survival. Bands are typically nomadic or semi-nomadic, and their social structure is relatively egalitarian.
Clan: Several bands united by a common ancestry, often forming larger kinship-based communities.
Tribe: A more complex social structure that includes multiple clans, usually settled in a particular geographic area. Tribes may have formalized leadership and a more specialized division of labor.
Chiefdom: A hierarchical social organization with a central chief or leader who holds authority over multiple tribes or groups.
State: The most advanced and complex form of social organization, characterized by a centralized government with defined territories, institutions, and a legal system. States typically have a monopoly on the use of force and maintain social order through laws and regulations

foreign land". *So rünami* is never used for mainland Indians. While it may sound comical, for a Naga to say "He is travelling to India" is perfectly understandable as someone who is travelling beyond the northeast to other parts of the country.

Many Nagas' first contact with Indians from Mainland India were army personnel carrying sophisticated weapons, killing, maiming, raping and burning granaries and houses of poor Naga villages.

The freedom struggle also gave rise and cemented the idea of Naga nationhood. Through their resistance and collective aspirations for autonomy, the Nagas developed a shared identity and vision distinct from other groups in the region. The movement unified diverse tribes, fostering a sense of solidarity and common purpose rooted in their cultural and historical uniqueness. This period not only intensified their pursuit of self-determination but also solidified the idea of a Naga nation, one that was grounded in preserving their heritage and governing themselves on their own terms.

It was in this era of conflict that Nagas were granted statehood under the Indian union. There were ramifications since it was a compromise. Nagas were demanding full sovereignty, often referred to as demand for a full rupee. The official position of the NNC starting with the Naga Club memorandum to the Simon Commission was that Nagas were never Indians. In the Naga Plebiscite of 1951, the percentage of Nagas who wanted to be free from the Indian union was 99%. Nagas, whether capable of sustaining a state structure or not, really believed in their right to self-determination. It was the geopolitical reality of the time that led the British to exit the Naga Hills and the Indian sub-continent in haste.

When statehood was granted to the Nagas, the features of modern democracy, including a formal bureaucracy, record-keeping, and the election of Members of the Legislative Assembly (MLAs), were introduced. This system was foreign to the Nagas, who had no prior experience with such centralized governance structures. While governance mechanisms were established and services began to be utilized, the government was often perceived as an external agency rather than an entity that naturally evolved from within the Naga society.

A result of this popular demand for sovereignty and the unfamiliarity with modern state institutions was the non-acceptance of governmental authority. This worked both ways: the government hesitated to assert power, while the people, in turn, did not recognize its authority.

For many years, the state government was largely perceived by the public as a provider of jobs and financial support rather than a system responsible for public service. This perception was so embedded that some even imagined the government as a benevolent figure. A person was supposed to have said: "I don't know who this government is, but he must be a very benevolent person." This outlook shaped the ambitions of educated individuals, who viewed government jobs as a path to secure, lifelong benefits. The goal was stability and financial support, rather than public duty or contribution. This perception created a peculiar dichotomy about employment: for the public, holding a government job implied one could receive a salary without substantial work, while not being a government employee was equated with being unemployed. This attitude reinforced a system in which government employees were valued for holding a position rather than for their work output. The belief that government employees need not fulfil their duties to receive pay fostered unprofessionalism and absenteeism in many departments, contributing to inefficiency within the government sector, where employees feel little pressure to perform their roles effectively. Take the case of a police constable as an illustration, applicable in many departments. To him "*Sahab* will call me if there is work". If there was no work, he could drink, gamble, go to fields, hunt, involve in church work or help the community organise different programs. The same *sahab* came to office once or twice a month when there were paper works to be filled as mandated by law. Ultimately, this culture led to governance that exists somewhat parallel to society rather than as an integrated system of service, with low expectations for accountability and engagement.

Another result of the popular demand for sovereignty and the unfamiliarity with modern state institutions was that an appreciation of how governance is financed through taxation did not emerge in the Naga consciousness. This could be attributed to a common Naga fear of taxation expressed in the memorandum to the Simon Commission, as also, an effort to placate the Nagas by the

Indian government. In conversing with this generation, one hears frequently on the liberal financial endowment "Nagas (cause for self-determination) could not stand in front of money" or "Indians have bought us with money".

It was also during this time that a system of patronage and clientelism developed. More educated individuals entered politics and were elected as Member of Legislative Assemblies (MLAs), initiating the tradition of providing jobs and financial assistance, which led to their veneration as benevolent leaders. Elected legislators, aiming to help themselves and others, learnt that by providing small amounts of money or resources, they could secure votes. While this practice was technically illegal, they found a way to circumvent the rules. The system of patronage and clientelism was an abuse of the communitarian ethos of helping out each other in exigencies. Traditionally, the Nagas had engaged in wealth redistribution through communal feasts and other means; giving money and resources began to be seen as another form of this redistribution. The key difference now was that legislators did not have to work hard for it; they simply drew from the resources provided by Delhi. Unfortunately, this was not characterised as corruption. In fact, the opposite happened. A person who did not provide jobs, contracts, and money to his constituents began to be seen as an impotent leader. The present author and Dr Venusa Tinyi, an assistant professor in the Department of Philosophy from University of Hyderabad, has written a research paper in which we called it a trilemma for a Naga leader – (a) the responsibility to be true to his office, (b) to help members of his clan, village, and tribe individually, (c) and to bring forth development for his constituency as a whole[5].

---

[5] Venusa Tinyi and Chothazo Nienu, "Making Sense of Corruption in Nagaland: A Culturalist Interpretation," in *Democracy in Nagaland: Tribes,*

In the same paper, the authors have compared Naga leaders to hunters. In traditional Naga communities, hunters would share their game. The more successful a hunter was, the more game he shared. A successful Naga leader was one who was able to hunt jobs and contracts successfully for his constituents. This is not very different from experiences in Papua New Guinea where when modern governmental institutions were introduced, tribal leaders fought with each other to bargain more resources for their tribes rather than for the welfare of the country as a whole.

Essential Insights 1.3 Patronage and Clientelism

Patronage and Clientelism

Patronage
The patronage system is a social and economic arrangement wherein individuals or entities in positions of power (patrons) provide support, benefits, or resources to others (clients) in exchange for services, loyalty, or political support. This system is often characterized by hierarchical or asymmetric power structures and is broader in scope compared to clientelism, encompassing various forms of support and influence.

Clientelism
Clientelism is a political and social system where powerful individuals or leaders provide material goods, services, or benefits to individuals or groups (clients) in exchange for political support, loyalty, or other forms of assistance. It is characterized by reciprocal relationships that often reinforce hierarchical structures.

Traditions, Tensions, ed. Jelle JP Wouters and Zhoto Tunyi (Kohima: Highlander Press, 2018), 159

> **Key Characteristics of Clientelism according to Allen Hicken[6]:**
>
> **Dyadic Relationships**: These are two-way interactions between patrons and clients, where both parties engage in reciprocal exchanges. The client receives benefits, while the patron gains political support or loyalty.
>
> **Contingency**: The delivery of goods or services is conditional upon the client fulfilling specific obligations, such as voting for a particular candidate or party. Without the client's action, the benefits are withheld.
>
> **Hierarchy**: The relationship is inherently unequal, with the politician, party, or broker holding a position of greater power and influence over the client, who relies on them for resources or favors.
>
> **Iteration**: These relationships are not limited to single transactions. Instead, they are continuous and ongoing, with repeated exchanges that reinforce the connection over time.

A friend of the author narrates an anecdote of a retired high ranking government officer from his village who was admonishing his villagers for proxy voting on election day. A fellow villager present in the queue reportedly silenced him "What did you do for the village while you were serving as the DGP (Director General of Police) that you are admonishing us now?" A person who followed the letter of the law did not necessarily earn the love of the people.

Contributions of the second generation

The state saw rapid transformation from village republics to modern state institutions. Naga mindset or institutions were

---

[6] Allen Hicken, "Clientelism," Annual Review of Political Science 14 (2011): 289–310, https://doi.org/10.1146/annurev.polisci.031908.220508

community-based while the unit of society for the government focuses on the individual. This generation was the connect between the village republics and modern state institutions. Their achievements were many:

It was they who learnt, borrowed, and developed the governance protocols.

This generation also developed the service rules governing services and cadres in varied roles in Nagaland at present.

This generation initiated the process of making public budgets, passing them and having them audited.

Many institutions were set up by this generation.

Development of both physical and non-physical infrastructure was another achievement.

Reformation from above

The introduction of modern institutions alongside statehood in Nagaland brought significant changes to the traditional systems of governance. However, this transition exposed the system to vulnerabilities due to the following factors:

Ignorance and Lack of Familiarity: The people of Nagaland, accustomed to their indigenous self-governing practices, were unfamiliar with the workings of modern political and administrative institutions. This lack of knowledge made the new system susceptible to misuse and exploitation.

Absence of Precedents: With no historical examples of how to adapt traditional governance structures to modern frameworks, there was no roadmap for implementation. This gap led to confusion and created opportunities for manipulation by those seeking personal gain.

Blatant Abuse by Self-Serving Individuals: Some individuals exploited the nascent system for personal benefit, taking advantage of the public's limited understanding of institutional processes. Corruption, nepotism, and favoritism became prevalent as checks and balances were either absent or weak.

Contradictions with Traditional Practices: Many rules and regulations introduced under modern governance directly contradicted long-standing Naga customs and traditions. This mismatch caused resistance among the people and further complicated the integration of modern systems.

Central Government's Measures to Address the Challenges

To address the weaknesses and bring stability to the system, the central government implemented various reforms gradually:

Role of Central Commissions in Reforming Nagaland: The first reform was the granting of universal adult franchise enabling women to have a say in the decision-making process through election of representative. The Election Commission of India ensured free and fair elections were conducted. Central commissions like the National Human Rights Commission and its counterpart at the state, the State Human Rights Commission, have addressed rights violations in Nagaland, while the Finance Commission has supported fiscal reforms. Bodies like the Union Public Service Commission and the University Grants Commission have promoted administrative and educational improvements.

Financial Incentives and Discipline: The central government provided financial aid and incentives to encourage institutional development and capacity-building. Investments have been made in infrastructure, education, and administration to strengthen the state's governance framework. The Reserve Bank of India (RBI) has had to discipline Nagaland for exceeding its overdraft limits and delaying repayment of Ways and Means Advances (WMA), imposing restrictions to enforce fiscal discipline and prevent excessive reliance on short-term borrowings.

Compulsion Through the Home Ministry: In some cases, the Home Ministry had to enforce compliance with central directives to ensure the implementation of reforms. This included measures to curb corruption, streamline administrative processes, and enhance accountability.

Essential Insights 1.4 Comparing the Characteristics of Bureaucracy and Tribal Society

Characteristics of a Bureaucracy	Features of Tribal Society
o Hierarchical structure with clearly defined levels of authority o Specialisation and division of labor among employees o Formal rules and regulations governing operations and decision-making o Impersonal and objective decision-making processes o Employment based on merit and qualifications o Clear lines of authority and accountability o Standardised procedures for handling routine tasks o Bureaucratic discretion within defined limits o Centralisation of decision-making at the top levels o Emphasis on efficiency, rationality, and predictability	Egalitarian Classlessness Communitarian - norms and ownership of properties Respect for elders over expertise Culture of Support and Assistance Close Family Ties

○ Written communication and record-keeping ○ Standardised recruitment and promotion processes ○ Emphasis on adherence to policies and procedures ○ Bureaucratic red tape and potential for bureaucratic inefficiency.	Limited Division of Labour Consensus decision making

Nagaland through the Eyes of the Third Generation

Nagas born from the late 1980s onward experienced a reality markedly different from the previous generation. Fractionalisation of Naga struggle for self-determination led to much bloodshed. This also revealed the worst tendencies of tribalism – the mutual suspicions of each other.

On a positive note, the economic reforms of 1991 brought sweeping changes across India, and their effects eventually reached Nagaland. With the economic reforms came greater access to foreign goods, cheaper products, and more choices. This generation witnessed the process of "creative destruction" inherent in a capitalist economy, where familiar and beloved brands like Lifebuoy soap, Surf and Nirma detergent gradually disappeared or lost prominence, replaced by newer alternatives, television channels grew from Doordarshan 1 and Doordarshan 2 to many channels (the many television channels are already being replaced by smart TV and streaming sites). Access to food and nutrition also improved over the years. Greater variety and availability of food items have contributed to better health and quality of life for Nagas.

The aspirations of Nagas have similarly evolved. In the 1990s, televisions became a staple in many households. This was followed by mobile phones in the early 2000s, spurred by Prime Minister Vajpayee's visit to Nagaland in 2003, when he facilitated the establishment of cellular networks. By the late 2000s, smartphones began to penetrate the market, and today, as disposable incomes rise, vehicles and other signs of prosperity are increasingly visible.

Factional violence—particularly instances of Nagas killing other Nagas—was a serious issue well into the early 2010s. Fortunately, such violence has significantly reduced and is almost nonexistent today, allowing society to focus more on growth and development.

Naga Cultural Advancement and Economic Frustrations

Nagaland's cultural identity has undergone significant transformation, blending traditional heritage with modern influences. The state has seen substantial advancement in fields such as modelling, sports, cuisine, music fusion and fashion.

The Nagas, like many tribal communities, however, are facing a cultural challenge, with parts of their heritage at risk of being lost. Some individuals and companies aim to promote and even commercialise aspects of Naga culture, though this can sometimes be exploitative. Meanwhile, Christianisation and secularisation have altered the context of many traditions, and younger generations are losing interest in them, adding to the risk of cultural loss. Economic incentives could help record, preserve, and develop these cultural elements. However, tribal organizations sometimes resist, fearing that creative changes will reduce cultural authenticity. While some aspects of culture are being reinterpreted, these remain limited. A thoughtful discussion is needed to balance respect for tradition with room for change.

Despite cultural advancements, economic frustrations persist. Many Nagas grapple with poor infrastructure, limited employment opportunities, and pervasive corruption. The Naga economy presents a stark contrast between visible displays of wealth and persistent infrastructural challenges. The sight of expensive SUVs navigating muddy, pothole-riddled roads reflects a paradox: the ownership of high-cost vehicles amid poor road conditions. Similarly, well-decorated weddings and grand functions often occur against a backdrop of an inconsistent power supply, where elaborate celebrations are juxtaposed with the unreliable infrastructure needed to support them. Furthermore, while picturesque Instagram posts showcase the region's scenic beauty and cultural richness, they obscure the daily reality of lack of basic amenities that communities face. Many young people excel in show business, with performances that would be the envy of performers even on stages like America's Got Talent; the same young people then have to manoeuvre potholes, muddy and dusty roads and low quality of life. Available jobs often offer very low wages, which fail to keep pace with the rising cost of living. Meanwhile, many government institutions—including schools, hospitals, and urban bodies—struggle to function effectively, leaving citizens without essential support.

Old Wine in New Bottle

Nagas are going through fast-paced transition. There is a broader acceptance of the state's authority, at the same time a change in expectations from the government. Just within a few years, recruitment rules have become more difficult to violate. There is also more transparency in awarding contracts. People in power are not expected to provide for their constituents and kith and kins as much as they were only a decade ago. Professionalism in government service has improved. Much reforms have taken place to make governance accessible to the people. There are still however, systemic issues that are difficult to overcome. Fundamentally, the state structure organises itself around the individual; Naga society is tribal and communitarian – this aspect of Naga society provide strength but at the same time weakens governance.

The society is metamorphosing between a community-centric society and an individualistic capitalistic society with a functioning modern government. In this metamorphosis, practices and customs of the past which were common and identified as good has transmute into the new system. Dr Jelle Wouters, an anthropologist who has worked closely in Nagaland called this "different Naga tribes, instead of adjusting themselves to modern democratic ideals, adjusted democracy to themselves[7]." While the immediate context in which this observation was made was with regard to voting behaviour among different tribes in Nagaland, one can extend the argument to other scenarios. It was Robert K Merton who observed "No earlier form of social organization ever gets truly abandoned or eliminated, and it always survives into the succeeding higher stages." Nagas have been transforming from identification with village republics to tribal identities to a broader Naga-consciousness. However, practices and beliefs of the past find their expression in the present. At times, these occur as contradictions or anomalies in the way governance is understood and society functions.

Identity-centric civil societies: The close community bond came about as a result of people spending time together. The new community groups are based on shared-identities. The organic nature of those communities has been lost. The assumptions for the formation of identity groups is Gemeinschaft (Communities) whereas their character is Gesellschaft (civil society).

Corruption and Nepotism: In a society where priority was given to kith and kins and community members, a government which was not

---

[7] Wouters, J.J.P. 2014. 'Performing democracy in Nagaland: past polities and present politics', Economic and Political Weekly, XLIX (16): 59-66.

financed from own taxation but through grants from Delhi, diverting those resources to kith and kins became easy. These diversion of resources came in the form of government jobs and government contracts. While these practices have reduced to a large extent, there is no doubt that the chances of a person being awarded lucrative government contracts and preferred place of posting still depends on a person's connections with people in positions of power.

Vote buying and selling. A rich person shared his resources during feasts of merits. This was even a moral obligation, and an honour he strove towards. Perhaps, where choices for showing off were minimal, this was the best avenue available for a person to make a name. The Feasts of Merit once played the role that status goods serve today – signalling that the person is wealthy. Where riches could not be acquired easily, organising a feast of merit revealed a person who worked hard, was diligent with resources, and enjoyed God's favour. In the closely-knit community, the resources even when spent this way was not wasted. In fact, opening one's house to others was seen as a way to attract blessings. A belief held among the Tenyimis was that if a person's granary seemed to run out quickly, the family could seek blessings for a well-stocked granary by organizing a small feast, typically among family members. Since a grand feast would be too expensive for everyone to organize, the small feast would include children (the idea being children do not eat as much as adults), with the hope that the presence of many people sharing a meal in the household would attract the blessings of a well-stocked granary. At present, one of the forms a culture of resource sharing has taken is vote buying and selling – a form of patron-client relationship.

Land ownership system: Land was plenty in proportion to the number of people. Nagaland's traditional land ownership system, characterised by communal, undefined titles, creates challenges like insecure property rights, barriers to development, and environmental strain, which hinder economic growth and equitable access to resources.

Patriarchy: In Nagaland, patriarchy shapes social structures, often limiting women's access to land, decision-making, and leadership roles, which affects gender equality and opportunities for women's empowerment.

Over the Horizon

It has been more than 60 years of Nagaland statehood. A lot of change has taken place in the six decades. The most important change is the broad acceptance of the state's authority though it has to be said that much state-building still needs to be done. A significant improvement is the public understanding of corruption. In the past, as mentioned, people who acquired public offices compete to distribute resources for their kith and kins. Those who refused or were unable to do so were labelled impotent, selfish, and unconcerning. However, a more blatant form of corruption has emerged now that people have become more enlightened about rules and regulations and office procedures. This involves deduction of funds allotted for development projects by elected members and government officials. Anecdotally, one hears from field workers funds being deducted even from beneficiaries of Direct Benefit Transfers by having the beneficiaries return them. The complain of government employees, which they also use to justify the fund embezzlement, is that the number of civil society organisations requesting funds is excessive. The civil societies take the name of the community (of which the government employees automatically become a member) making refusal to pay difficult. To curb excessive fund-raising activities, fund-raising activities have even been banned in certain places. The formation of organisations and complains about contributions to fund them is a dynamic to watch out for in the coming decade.

The Naga society has much economic potentials in areas such as ecotourism, cultural tourism, and commercial agriculture. Urbanisation as a multiplier for economic growth though understood by the public, has not been backed by enough investment on hard infrastructure. Nagaland urban centres are not immune to urbanisation constraints such as high land prices, congestions, unaffordable housing, and difficulty to provide basic amenities. However, urbanisation in Nagaland suffer from an additional problem of refusal to sell resources by communities surrounding the urban centres severely constraining their growth potential and leading to the development of an underlying "broken window[8]" economy, the best example of which is water.

Complicating matters is the existence of many Naga political groups, serving as a Sword of Damocles, with the potential for bloodshed any given day. It is the "problem child of the family" serving as the excuse for any malaise in Nagaland. Naga political problem is similar to the error term in statistics, unknown in scientific theory, and an act of god in insurance. So long as the political problem exists, there will always be uncertainty in Nagaland. This is not to say that solving the political problem will usher in a golden era of peace, stability and development. Other issues such as institutional path

---

[8] When a person breaks a glass window, it creates job for the window repairer. Breaking a window is thus beneficial! Keynesian economics calling for government spending, is at times, criticised as using this logic. The person whose window was broken cannot now spend money on buying new cloths, foregoing the income of the tailor. Supplying water to Kohima through water tanks create jobs for drivers and mechanics who have to repair vehicles. However, it reduces disposable income of consumers. The overall effect is a loss on the state capital.

dependency, low state capacity and low trust in state as an allocator of resources will continue to hinder development.

2

Article 371A

How would you answer?

Do you think Article 371A is holding Nagas back?

Can Article 371A be used to reject any aspect of Indian constitution saying it violates Naga customary law?

Elaborate the meaning "land and its resources". Does the word "resources" missing from Article 371G (Mizoram) carry any significance?

Elaborate Nagaland Petroleum and Natural Gas Rules, 2012.

Discussion

Article 371A[9] for this chapter will be studied under two major heads:

---

[9] Article 371A

 Special provision with respect to the State of Nagaland.

(1) Notwithstanding anything in this Constitution,

1. The question about land and its resources
2. The issue on customary laws

It has to be noted that there is no clarity on many of the issues surrounding Article 371A. The best an aspirant can do is to be aware of the different claimants and issues surrounding the article. At times, fear is also expressed that Article 371A would go the way of Article 370 – the article providing special provisions for the erstwhile state of Jammu and Kashmir. This is true of both land and its resources and customary law. On land and its resources, because of complications that would arise, all the actors vis the central government, the Nagaland Government and the landowners do not want to rock the boat, leading to the existence of lawlessness in managing mineral resources in the state. Each actor could lay claim to resources based on laws and legal principles that already exist. However, assertion by one would lead to conflict with the others. On customary law, the issue of Uniform Civil Code (UCC) being forced down on tribal communities such as Nagas is a fear often expressed. The Indian right uses Uniform Civil Code as a political tool to alienate Muslims and unite Hindus. The other issue of UCC as a progressive

---

(a) no Act of Parliament in respect of

i) religious or social practices of the Nagas,

ii) Naga customary law and procedure,

(iii) administration of civil and criminal justice involving decisions according to Naga customary law,

(iv) ownership and transfer of land and its resources, shall apply to the State of Nagaland unless the Legislative Assembly of Nagaland by a resolution so decides;

tool to uplift women and other sections of society is often ignored in such a discourse.

The questions about land and its resources

The following passage explores the interpretation of Article 371A, particularly the critical distinction between "land" and "land and its resources." It examines how "land" is understood in economics, its constitutional context, the perspective of the signatories of the 16-Point Agreement, the central government's authority over mineral resources, the role of customary rights in mineral ownership, the experience of Nagaland Legislative Assembly vis-à-vis Nagaland Petroleum and Natural Gas Rules, 2012, and the disputes surrounding the ownership of mineral resources in Nagaland.

In economics textbooks, the term "land" refers to all natural resources used in the production process. This includes not only physical land but also resources like minerals, forests, water, and air. It encompasses everything found in nature that is not created by human effort and can be used to produce goods and services.

However, under the Indian Constitution, the term "land" has a narrower and more specific interpretation compared to its broad economic meaning. In legal terms, "land" primarily refers to the rights and ownership of immovable property, including the surface of the earth, any structures built on it, and the subsoil. Land in this context is also connected to issues of land tenure, ownership, and regulation, particularly under the state's jurisdiction.

According to the Constitution, "land" falls under the State List (List II, Schedule 7), giving state governments authority to legislate on matters such as land rights, land revenue, tenancy, and land reforms. This narrower legal interpretation focuses on property rights, acquisition, and land use rather than encompassing all natural resources as in economic theory.

Meaning of Land and its Resources in the 16-Point Agreement

The original text of Clause 7 in the 16-Point Agreement[10] only uses the phrase "land and its resources" without elaborating the meaning of what resources mean. In an article published in the Nagaland Post, SC Jamir [11] explained its meaning during the negotiations, showing that "land and its resources" was understood to include "all minerals and mineral resources, including petroleum and its bye-products [sic]."

Jamir links this interpretation to the Nine-Point Agreement of 1947, which stipulated that "land with all its resources in the Naga Hills should not be alienated to a non-Naga without the consent of the Naga National Council." This principle was carried over into the 16-Point Agreement and reflected in Article 371(A) of the Indian Constitution. Article 371(A) ensures that no parliamentary law regarding the "ownership and transfer of land and its resources" would apply to Nagaland without the approval of the state's Legislative Assembly.

---

[10] The 16-Point Agreement: https://www.satp.org/satporgtp/countries/india/states/nagaland/documents/papers/nagaland_16point.htm#:~:text=2.,of%20the%20Government%20of%20Nagaland.

[11] SC Jamir, "Sanctity of Article 371A, Sub-clause (iv) Land and Its Resources", *Nagaland Post*, May 9, 2023,

https://nagalandpost.com/index.php/2023/05/09/sanctity-of-article-371a-sub-clause-iv-land-and-its-resources/

Jamir further explains that the term "resources" refers to those "linked with, emanating from, and inherent/imbedded in land." This covers not only the surface but also the minerals, petroleum, and other non-renewable resources beneath it. He recalls "everyone present that day in 1960 was certain" that the phrase "land and its resources" included these elements, ensuring Nagaland's control over them unless otherwise decided by the state itself.

Central Government Authority over Mineral Resources

According to Article 246 of the Indian Constitution, Parliament has exclusive powers to make laws concerning matters listed in List I (the Union List) of the Seventh Schedule. Item 54 of this list gives Parliament control over the regulation of mines and mineral development, allowing the central government to legislate on the ownership, exploration, and extraction of mineral resources when they are declared to be of national importance. This means that the central government's authority over resources like petroleum, coal, iron, and other minerals is dominant over state regulations.

A key piece of legislation supporting this is the Mines and Minerals (Regulation & Development) Act, 1957. This Act lays the foundation for regulating and developing India's mineral resources. It gives the central government powers to issue licenses and leases for the mining of major minerals and provides a framework for scientific development, conservation, and the prevention of resource misuse. Under this Act, states have limited control, mainly restricted to regulating minor minerals, while the central government retains control over major minerals such as coal, iron, and petroleum.

The central government's overarching control is intended to ensure that minerals of national importance are developed and conserved in a way that benefits the country as a whole. **However, in cases where specific land ownership or customary rights are recognized, these powers do not apply automatically**. For example, in the Malabar case (specifically Threesiamma Jacob & Others vs. Geologist, Department of Mining & Geology & Others), the Supreme Court ruled that private landowners in Kerala's Malabar region, holding ryotwari pattas, had ownership of minerals beneath their land, unless the State had explicitly taken away such rights through law. The ruling emphasized that Article 294 (dealing with State ownership of property) did not automatically make the State the owner of minerals under private land. This judgment highlights the complexities of mineral ownership and how customary or historical land ownership systems can challenge the central government's rights to minerals.

Exemption for Nagaland under Article 371A?

According to Moatoshi Ao [12], a legal authority on Naga customary law, in contrast to the general application of Article 246, Article 371A of the Constitution grants Nagaland special protections that exempt it from the automatic application of central laws relating to land and resources. This article specifically recognizes the customary rights of the Naga people regarding land ownership and the transfer of resources, meaning that any Act of Parliament related to land or natural resources does not apply to Nagaland unless the Legislative Assembly of Nagaland consents to it.

As a result, central laws like the Petroleum Act, 1934, the Oilfields (Regulation & Development) Act, 1948, the Mines and Minerals (Regulation & Development) Act, 1957, and the Inflammable Substances Act, 1952 are not automatically enforceable in Nagaland. These Acts regulate the extraction and handling of petroleum, minerals, and flammable substances across India, but their enforcement in Nagaland requires the state government's

---

[12] Moatoshi Ao, "Naga Customary Law Vis-à-Vis the Advent of Administration: Historical Legal Framework and Impact on Adjudication," Journal of the Campus Law Centre (2014): 162–184.

approval, recognizing the customary land ownership and resource transfer rights protected by Article 371A.

The State of Nagaland even attempted to create its own framework for regulating resources through the Nagaland Petroleum & Natural Gas Regulations, 2012. The Government of Nagaland came up with this legislation after consulting prominent legal scholars who agreed that major minerals are under the remit of the Nagaland Legislative Assembly as provided under Article 371A[13].

However, the Nagaland Petroleum & Natural Gas Regulations, 2012 faced resistance from the central government's Ministry of Petroleum and Natural Gas as a legislation outside the state's legislative assembly's jurisdiction. The Nagaland Government in turn called the civil societies in the state for discussion on the issue. The issue of balancing Nagaland's autonomy with the central government's desire to regulate resources on a national scale is thus quite complex.

Who has control over resources found on land - the landowners or the state government?

Another question regarding land and its resources is who controls the mineral resources found on land. Among the Nagas, there are primarily two claimants[14]:

---

[13] H. Kham Khan Suan, "Adding Fuel to the Fire" The Hindu, last updated July 10, 2016, https://www.thehindu.com/opinion/lead/adding-fuel-to-the-fire/article5004098.ece

[14] The tribal apex hohos and village councils seek to influence decisions regarding the distribution of mineral resources, whereas landowners resist such interference, aiming to retain exclusive control. One can add Naga political groups and other civil societies that seek to influence decisions regarding the distribution of mineral resources. However, the words "primarily two claimants" (emphasis here is two) is being used since the landowners and the Government of Nagaland are the two major entities.

1.   The Nagaland Government and

2.   Landowners

The argument of the landowners is that since Article 371A protects Naga customary law when it comes to ownership of land and its resources, the Naga customary recognises their rights as landowners. As such, the mineral resources should belong to them exclusively. The Nagaland Legislative Assembly, as the highest legislative authority in the state, believes it has the legislative rights to legislate on mineral resources.

Nagaland Petroleum and Natural Gas Rules, 2012 legislated under provisions of Article 371A however, recognises three types of landowners[15]:

i)   Individuals
ii)   Village Council
iii)   State Government

Nagaland Petroleum and Natural Gas Rules, 2012 thus have a broader interpretation of landowners.

Article 371A vs Article 371G

An important detail many miss out while discussing Article 371A is the similarity between Article 371A and Article 371G[16]. The two

---

[15] H. Kham Khan Suan, "Adding Fuel to the Fire" The Hindu, last updated July 10, 2016, https://www.thehindu.com/opinion/lead/adding-fuel-to-the-fire/article5004098.ece

[16] 371G: Special provision with respect to the State of Mizoram.

Notwithstanding anything in this Constitution,:

(a) no Act of Parliament in respect of:

i) religious or social practices of the Mizos,

articles are word for word identical except in clause a (iv). Where it says "land and its resources" for Nagaland; for Mizoram, it is limited to "land". Whether the additional word "resources" has any significance merits exploration.

Article 371A and Naga Customary Law

India operates under a system of weak legal pluralism, where the modern legal system and customary laws coexist, but the modern legal framework is generally given precedence. Under this model, while customary laws are acknowledged, they are often subordinate to statutory or codified laws, especially when conflicts arise. In contrast, strong legal pluralism would mean that both customary and modern laws hold equal authority, with neither automatically taking precedence over the other. This contrast is critical to understanding the place of Article 371A of the Indian Constitution, which grants special autonomy to the state of Nagaland in respect of Naga customary laws, religious practices, and social customs.

Recognition of Customary Law in the Constitution

Although Article 371A is unique in that it grants Nagaland a high degree of autonomy over its cultural and legal practices, it is important to recognize that it is not an isolated case. Other sections of Indian society also have their customary rights and traditions protected in the Constitution and legal frameworks. For example:

(ii) Mizo customary law and procedure,

(iii) administration of civil and criminal justice involving decisions according to Mizo customary law,

(iv) ownership and transfer of land, shall apply to the State of Mizoram unless the Legislative Assembly of the State of Mizoram by a resolution so decides.

Article 13 recognizes that customary law can have legal force unless it is inconsistent with the fundamental rights guaranteed by the Constitution. This provision indirectly acknowledges that custom can be a source of law, albeit within certain limits.

The Fifth Schedule (Article 244) provides special provisions for the governance of Scheduled Areas, where the Governor has the authority to make regulations that can modify or exclude the application of laws to protect tribal interests, indirectly supporting the preservation of customary laws. The Sixth Schedule (Article 244A), on the other hand, directly empowers Autonomous District Councils in certain tribal areas to govern themselves and administer justice according to their customary laws, giving explicit protection to these traditional practices. Both schedules aim to safeguard the unique legal and cultural rights of indigenous communities.

Section 13 of the Indian Evidence Act, 1872[17] permits the use of custom as a basis for determining ownership, especially in disputes involving land and property in areas where written laws may not provide the full picture of societal practices.

Furthermore, several provisions of the The Code of Criminal Procedure, 1973 (CrPC)[18] do not apply to Nagaland and tribal Areas, recognizing that these regions often function under their own traditional legal systems.

---

[17] The Bharatiya Nyaya Sanhita, 2023, Section 11 replicates Section 13 of the Indian Evidence Act, 1872, allowing custom to be used as a basis for determining ownership, particularly in land and property disputes where written laws may not capture the full scope of societal practices.

[18] Bharatiya Nagarik Suraksha Sanhita (BNSS), 2023 replicates provision of The Code of Criminal Procedure, 1973 (CrPC) that excludes Nagaland and other tribal areas.

Customary laws in India, including those in Nagaland, bear a resemblance to English common law in their reliance on community norms, tradition, and precedent. However, for many indigenous communities, the fight to retain their customary laws is deeply tied to broader issues of self-determination and cultural preservation. Customary law is not merely a legal issue but a central part of the identity and autonomy of these communities. In Nagaland, the ongoing effort to maintain customary laws can be seen as a broader struggle for political and cultural recognition, rooted in the state's distinct history and sociopolitical identity[19].

Advantages of Customary Laws

Customary laws are deeply rooted in the traditions and values of communities, ensuring their relevance and acceptability among the people they govern.

These laws are flexible, allowing adaptation to specific local contexts and fostering social cohesion.

They also promote alternative dispute resolution mechanisms, such as mediation and arbitration, which are often quicker and less adversarial than formal judicial processes.

Foundation of Naga Customary Law

In the case of Naga customary law, there are two key foundations:

Spiritual Belief: Central to Naga life is the belief in God or divine justice, which places a high value on oaths. When a person swears an oath, it is seen as binding, with the final judgment left to

---

[19] Lue Htar, Myat The Thitsar, and Helene Maria Kyed, Why Is Customary Law So Strong? Political Recognition and Justice Practices in the Naga Self-Administered Zone (Copenhagen: Danish Institute for International Studies, October 6, 2020).

divine providence. Oaths are treated with the utmost seriousness, and once taken, the matter is often considered resolved in the eyes of the community.

Close-knit Community Structure: The communal nature of Naga society emphasizes values such as honour, truth, hard work, and valour. In such a tightly knit society, where good reputation carries significant influence, forms of punishment like excommunication or public shaming were highly effective in maintaining social order.

Societal Change and Challenges to Naga Customary Law

Conflicting Laws: The lack of precise guidelines in Article 371-A creates confusion between state and customary justice.

Women's Rights: Gender biases exist, such as the exclusion of women from participating in the decision-making process within customary courts. Gender discrimination remains one of the most contested aspects of Naga customary laws. In many cases, these laws tend to disadvantage women in matters such as inheritance, divorce, child custody, and maintenance, often adhering to patriarchal norms that limit women's rights. There is a growing consensus that reforms are necessary to address these inequalities. Specific areas where customary laws have been criticized include:

Divorce and Marital Rights: Women often face significant disadvantages in divorce proceedings under customary law.

Domestic Violence and Marital Rape: These issues remain under-addressed in traditional legal frameworks.

Justice and Power: Customary law enforcement can sometimes be influenced by power dynamics and public opinion, potentially leading to misuse.

Oath-Taking as a Legal Mechanism: Reliance on oaths as the final arbiter of truth is increasingly seen as an outdated practice that can no longer meet the standards of modern justice systems.

Naga Tribunal and Customary Law in Nagaland?[20]

The idea of establishing a Naga Tribunal has emerged as a potential path to unify and standardize customary laws within Nagaland, providing a comprehensive legal structure that respects cultural traditions while adapting to modern societal needs. One proposed approach is the creation of a written constitution that outlines what constitutes customary law and the remedies available. This process would involve multidisciplinary expertise, including scientists, anthropologists, and lawyers, to avoid potential confusion that might arise from transcribing oral traditions and to navigate the complexity of varied customary practices among different tribes.

There is also recognition that the legislative body should develop a uniform set of rules to address the changing dynamics of society. This approach would acknowledge the significant role of customary laws while ensuring they evolve to meet contemporary expectations.

A critical foundation for this concept lies in the provisions of the 16 Point Agreement, particularly those addressing local self-governance and the administration of justice. These provisions suggest that local councils, which have traditionally handled tribal matters, could escalate cases to a broader 'Naga Tribunal' covering the entire state to oversee matters concerning customary law. This tribunal could act as an apex body to streamline practices, propose amendments, and maintain a clear distinction from the legislative

---

[20] What Is Customary Law for the Nagas?" Morung Express, February 23, 2017, Dimapur, https://morungexpress.com/what-customary-law-nagas

body, thus preserving the separation between legislative and judicial functions.

However, challenges remain. There is a concern that while similarities exist among customary laws, regional variations have led to unique practices, making it difficult to unify them under one umbrella. This suggests that while a Naga Tribunal is feasible, it would require careful consideration to address these regional differences.

A significant point of contention is the inclusion of women in traditional legal processes. Historically excluded from customary arbitration, women have demonstrated their effectiveness in legal and judicial roles within the formal state systems. The question arises: should efforts be made to integrate women into customary law practices? It is argued that this transformation depends on the support and active involvement of both men and women within the community. Without their consensus, change may be difficult to implement. The exclusion of women from decision-making bodies contradicts the fundamental notion of justice that customary law aims to uphold.

It has been noted that resistance to inclusion may be strong due to the powerful influence of tribe-based organizations. To move forward, discussions within each tribe are necessary to consider updating customary laws, a process that could be facilitated by the state government. The change should involve both top-down and bottom-up approaches to ensure that the collective wisdom of both genders contributes to these updates. This approach would create a foundation capable of supporting a Naga Tribunal that embodies mutual understanding and inclusivity.

Although establishing a Naga Tribunal may face significant challenges due to deeply rooted traditions and diverse laws, its potential benefits—fostering unity and adapting justice to modern needs—could serve as an important step toward transforming customary law from a source of conflict into an integral part of communal life.

Do you think Article 371A is holding Nagas back?

Article 371A is similar to an insurance policy for the Nagas. Often people who has good insurance coverage become complacent in taking care of their health. When we compare statements of Chief Ministers of Nagaland with other northeastern states or the statements of Nagaland's representatives in the Indian parliament, we see our representatives been very docile. At other times, reforms brought by the Indian parliament which do not have anything to do with Article 371A have been delayed citing the article. An argument can be made that Article 371A has made Nagas complacent. However, Nagas are very different from mainland Indians and the insurance policy in the form of Article 371A is needed.

With recent developments on carbon trading, 371A protecting tribal property rights could bring much foreign exchange revenue through forests in Nagaland acting as carbon sinks.

Can Article 371A be used to reject any aspect of Indian constitution saying it violates Naga customary law?

The Supreme Court stated in Minerva Mills Case (1980), "the donee of a limited power cannot use that power and give itself unlimited power." An argument can be made that Article 371A cannot go beyond what is provided in the state list and concurrent list. When Naga customary practices are in violation of Fundamental Rights, certainly, the Supreme Court or the Parliament will step in.

Elaborate the meaning "land and its resources" under Article 371A. Does the word "resources" missing from Article 371G (Mizoram) carry any significance?

There is ambiguity to the meaning land and its resources under 371A. The Nagaland Legislative Assembly is of the position that the term means land and the resources that are found in it including mineral resources such as oil, coal, etc. Accordingly, it passed the Nagaland Petroleum and Natural Gas Rules, 2012. An opinion article from *the Hindu* says the Government of Nagaland made this legislation after consulting top lawyers over several years who all agreed that the term "resources" under 371A include mineral resources. However, mineral resources come under the Union List where only the parliament is the competent authority to pass legislation. Accordingly, the central Ministry of Petroleum and Natural Gas had opposed the legislation.

Whether the term "resources" missing from Article 371G has any significance or not has not been explored by anyone as per my knowledge.

Elaborate Nagaland Petroleum and Natural Gas Rules, 2012.

The Nagaland Petroleum and Natural Gas Rules, 2012 were established to create a framework for inviting bids from oil companies through Expressions of Interest (EoI) for exploration rights in the state. The rules outlined that successful companies would be granted the right to explore and extract oil, with the condition that a percentage of the revenue generated would be allocated to the state government and invested in local infrastructure, such as schools and hospitals. However, these rules faced significant opposition from landowners, who argued that Article 371A of the Indian Constitution implicitly recognizes the traditional land ownership system, which prioritises the rights of the landowners over the state government.

3

Communitisation

How would you answer?

What is Communitisation?

Are there conceptual inconsistencies with Communitisation? Or are there weaknesses in Communitisation?

What suggestions would you recommend the government on Communitisation?

What is School Management Committee? What is the role of SMC vis-a-vis VEC?

What is social capital? Is it relevant to Communitisation?

What is the connection between Village Development Boards or Village Councils and Communitisation?

Which has been more successful - VDBs or Communitisation and why?

Do you see any fundamental problem with Communitisation as a governance model?

Discussion

Communitisation can be defined as an institutional arrangement in which the government has transferred the ownership and responsibility of management of government services and utility system to the community. In this case, the community is the village community, and the government services and utility system consist of seven sectors as provided in the Communitisation Act, 2002: education, health, power, forest, roads, sanitation, and other welfare and development matters.

Communitisation was pioneered by RS Pandey, the then Chief Secretary of Government of Nagaland who wanted to tap the social capital of the Naga villages. The reasoning behind the introduction of Communitisation was the observation that Naga government institutions were not performing efficiently and that Nagas possessed strong social capital.

Communitisation is different from the commonly known Public-Private Partnership (PPP) in that PPP consist of a government firm been transferred to the management of another private firm who is not necessarily the user whereas Communitisation consist in transferring the government institution been transferred to the user community while the employees continue to be employees of the government.

In his book 'Communitisation: the third way of governance', RS Pandey lay out his vision of the working of Communitisation. Communitisation is based on a triple 'T' approach:

T: Trust the Community

T: Transfer the resources and management to the community

T: Train the Community

The reasoning of Communitisation is to trust the user community to enforce order to run institutions smoothly. Since community members are the users of the government service and utility delivery system, they will ensure that institutions perform efficiently. The community can contribute resources to enhance the functioning of the government service infrastructure. Where needed, the village community can contribute their expertise in running the institutions. A whole new vision of government service is envisioned where the needs of the people are not only kept at the centre but that people can also contribute to the strengthening of institutions not only through their material and non-material contributions but also in envisioning new pathways for those institutions. Thus, government institutions are no longer alien structures that exist to serve the community but are an organic part of the community.

Social Capital as the fuel for Communitisation

Social capital refers to the networks, relationships, and norms that enable individuals and groups to work together more effectively to achieve common goals. It encompasses the trust, cooperation, and mutual support that arise from social interactions within a community, organization, or society. Social capital can manifest in various forms, such as bonding capital (strong ties within a close-knit group), bridging capital (connections between diverse groups), and linking capital (relationships across different levels of power or social hierarchy). High levels of social capital can lead to improved social cohesion, economic development, and overall well-being, while a lack of social capital can result in social fragmentation and reduced collective efficacy.

Assessment of Communitisation

Communitisation has a mixed track record. Strangely, intellectuals so far are not willing to call out the weaknesses inherent in Communitisation. Usually, researchers who have done research on Communitisation espoused the virtues of Communitisation. On the other hand, government officials and stakeholders of government institutions have a different opinion about Communitisation i.e. they are frustrated that Communitisation has not worked and that it should be reviewed. This calls for a thorough analysis of the strengths and weaknesses of Communitisation and the contradictory positions of different actors.

Why Communitisation is appreciated

Communitisation as a concept is highly admirable. In a world where governments' powers and responsibilities are multiplying, trusting the community to have a stake in their own governance sounds idealistic and workable. Indeed, in the first few years of Communitisation, the empowerment work wonderfully. This is best reflected in the book "VEC Speak" brought out by the Education Department where the virtues of Communitisation were filled with praise in each page[21]. Praise for the program however consistently mentioned improvement in financial aspect from the education department. As Zavise Rume, an educationist at the State Council of Education and Research Training, told this author in an interview, "Communitisation had a fortunate simultaneous launching with Sarva Shiksha Abhiyan. The message of the central government then was: 'Do not worry about money, your only care should be that the program work successfully.'" In the field of education, money was used to hire local community elders to teach children in government schools crafts that were been forgotten, with the department under

---

[21] *VEC Speak*, published by the Directorate of School Education, Nagaland (Kohima, 2004)

close scrutiny when Communitisation was launched, funds were given properly to schools, mid day meals became regular, and books were distributed to students in fulfilment of free education commitments. Single Point Metering for the whole village led to increased household power consumption without repercussion for high power bills. Villagers posted health workers from their own villages to work at their places arresting to an extent absentee health workers.

The honeymoon phase however soon ended. Communitisation faced a principal-agent problem where the principal (community) had no control over the agent (government employees). In theory, the community owned the government institutions. However, the ownership did not translate to any meaningful control or oversight. Over the years, several problems became evident with Communitisation – the concept itself, the changing nature of Naga society, and the mismatch with bureaucratic process.

Conceptual problems inherent within Communitisation itself

i)   Community definition

Within Communitisation, there are multiple layers of the term 'community'. At times, it identifies community as village community whereas at other times, the community implies 'user community'. While the village community is often seen as a composite whole, and this is true in several cases, a person's identification with his village community is not always strong. Thus, the assumption of Communitisation that the user community would ensure smooth running of institutions and service delivery do not always work since not everyone in the village is a user. Naga villages, by virtue of their social interactions in the past, were identified as one. Nagas are undergoing changes with people migrating to urban regions for better education, lifestyles and employment, politics also disrupts the village bond, and income and education disparities have led to the development of social hierarchy.

ii)   Communitisation as confrontation

Government schoolteachers in villages often complain that villagers do not work with a spirit of cooperation but approach the teachers with an attitude to confront them without understanding the intricacies of the school environment. Health workers also convey the same problem: "villagers do not understand the constraints and the limited supply given by the government."

Communitisations' Failure from Government weaknesses

I.   No Training - the third T

The Government of Nagaland has not kept its part of the bargain in not conducting trainings for stakeholders in the system. Without training on the vision of Communitisation, office procedures, school administration, and community mobilisation villagers are left handicapped.

II.   No books and other materials on time

The school education department also has not been able to provide materials to schools on time. This leads to hampering of the smooth day-to-day functioning of the schools. The funds released for day-to-day functioning of the schools such as buying chalks, dusters, co-curricular activities are released haphazardly year to year such that teachers cannot make plans to run the schools. The same criticism is applicable to other sectors where Communitisation is in place.

Communitisation's Failure Due to Societal Challenges

Communitisation faces significant challenges stemming from societal dynamics. In less developed areas, the financial and material limitations of the community, along with the lack of active parental involvement in children's education, hinder the effective functioning of schools. Additionally, reforms like streamlining salaries to prevent extortion by Naga political groups have weakened community-led accountability mechanisms, such as the role of Village Education Committees (VECs).

I.　　Villages in Less Developed Areas

The education department expects the community members to contribute materially to the functioning of the schools as part of Communitisation. However, in many villages, the poorest children continue to be sent to government schools. The parents of these children can at the most contribute a few material items such as bamboo, firewood, and vegetables (for mid-day meal) and sacrifice a few days a year in cleaning the campus of the school. However, beyond that they cannot do much. A proper functioning of schools also requires strong interest in their children's education at home. When proper care is not provided at home, it leads to poor learning, dwindling attendance and dropouts. When children from dysfunctional families are sent to government schools, it takes a lot of motivation for both the teachers and the students – for teachers to teach and for children to continue their education. Often, children lose motivation to study and leave schools midway.

The Government of India through its Ayushman Bharat scheme has initiated a system of tracking beneficiaries, where medicines and other accessories used have to be recorded on its health portal for better service delivery and planning. However, villages facing poor network connectivity faces significant challenges.

At times, the small number of health workers is also stretched. Village health centers are also supplied with medicines that are close to expiration, leaving no room for long-term planning and storage.

Villages in remote areas often experience power cuts due to supply shortages or weather-related damage to power lines. Without a steady power supply, the question of power management becomes irrelevant.

## II.	Underground Problem or Naga Political Groups

Initially, the principle of 'No-work, No-pay' was implemented by requiring the signatures of VEC for teachers' salary to be drawn. This served as an accountability measure on the attendance of the teachers in the schools. However, salaries of teachers had to be streamlined through the banks due to demands by different political groups in the state of a share of the teachers' salaries. The streamlining of government employees' salaries was also part of a bigger reform move from the government. The reform effectively stripped VECs of their authority, rendering them powerless.

Successful Communitised Villages

There are villages where Communitisation has been a major success. Schools close to urban centers such as Viswema, Jotsoma and Jakhama have been very successful. The VEC chairmen of these villages are highly accomplished individuals. They are able to mobilise the community to contribute funds to the schools and ensure that schools are functioning smoothly. Since these villages are richer compared to most of the villages in Nagaland, people can contribute meaningfully without their finances being pinched.

An unintended consequence of Communitisation is thus more inequality as more developed, better educated and more organised communities are able to organise themselves better. This is in keeping with findings from other studies on community related programs.

Communitisation and High Power Bills to the Government

The Communitisation of power distribution in village communities has led to over consumption of power and not enough revenue being generated to meet the consumption needs. The government is thus subsiding the consumption of power in Nagaland. Funnily, this is not a subsidy the government is gladly undertaking. The government sees the deficit revenue as a loophole rather than a positive subsidy. Since rich people consumes more power, the subsidy is inefficient in that it is being showered on people who do not need it. Village leaders are opposed to removing Communitisation in power sector because of the benefits its constituents are receiving. For sustainable development, the state has no choice but to review the system of metering the whole village and introduce a single individual user-pay basis where each household pays what they have consumed, as is being carried out. [As of this writing, the government has repealed Communitisation of Power in urban areas. Single Point Metering for the whole village has been removed. Smart metering for all rural consumers has been initiated.]

Village Development Boards (VDB) and Village Councils (VC) and Communitisation

VDBs and VCs in Nagaland have been very successful in bringing grassroots empowerment. The government has integrated successfully the VDB and VC into its governance structure. Dedicated funds and government machinery thus exist to work along with VDB and VC. The VDB and VC have an organic existence in that Naga villages not a long time ago were village republics, independent of each other. When Communitisation was initiated, it was expected that Communitisation would also become integral to the governance of government institutions with the community playing an active role. This has not been the case in most of the villages in Nagaland. There are several reasons:

1. **Dedicated funds are not allotted to Communitisation.** Leaders serving the villages in different capacities under Communitisation have to spend from their own pocket for works related to the village. This is not sustainable for many poor people serving as VEC leaders. The Communitisation Act, 2002 has a section on funds to be granted to communitised bodies. However, dedicated funds are not set aside for Communitisation in the government budgets passed each year.

2. **Original Structure of Communitised Departments do not envision outside intervention**

The communitised departments can function without the intervention of the village community since they have dedicated employees in each position. For integrating with the village communities, the departments would have to create space in their bureaucratic hierarchy or in their work calendars to accommodate the concerns of the village community. Governments structures in Nagaland (and the wider India) are hierarchical, rigid and specialised. In fact, bureaucracies are largely hierarchical, rigid and specialised by their very nature. Integrating the village community into the bureaucratic hierarchy, for the stakeholders, is like fitting square pegs into round holes. Each government department operates with service rules for its employees, along with clearly defined tasks for both the department and individual employees. For bureaucrats occupying a bureaucratic position, Communitisation is a nuisance to those specialised roles.

State Institutions and Communitisation

Communitisation sought to fix the day-to-day non-functioning of government institutions. These institutions have strong institutional memories which cannot be erased easily. A highly spirited superior trying to fix delinquencies will be seen as over smart, a scenario where the person trying to correct a wrong is seen in bad light. The government as an institution is still young in Nagaland. It will take combined concerted efforts from the government and the public to fix non-functioning institutions.

Model Answers

What is Communitisation?

Communitisation is an institutional arrangement in which the government has transferred the ownership and responsibility of management of government services and utility system to the community. In this case, the community is the village community, and the government services and utility system consist of education, health, power, sanitation, roads, forests and other welfare and development matters.

Communitisation was made possible through the Communitisation act, 2002. It was pioneered by RS Pandey, the then Chief Secretary of Government of Nagaland who sought to tap the social capital of the Naga villages. The reasoning behind the introduction of Communitisation was the observation that Naga government institutions were not performing efficiently.

There are weaknesses inherent within the very concept of Communitisation. The first is the different layers of communities that exist not defined properly by Communitisation. Communitisation regards user community and village community interchangeably with the understanding that the village community is the user community. This is not necessarily the case. Secondly, integrating the village community into the bureaucratic hierarchy would require creating space in the service rules or departmental modalities. This has not taken place. Communitisation thus sticks out like a sore thumb. Thirdly, the Training aspect of Communitisation has not been followed through by the government. The village community has no mechanism for that redressal.

What suggestions would you recommend the government?

The government needs a thorough revision of Communitisation. Communitisation should not be scrapped because communities where they are working wonderfully would suffer. However, the government should consider integrating the VEC into the education department similar to the way the BDO works with the VDB and the district administration works with the VC. The government should also streamline the functioning of VECs. Simply stating that it should ensure that schools are run properly doesn't make sense since the headmaster of the school is doing that job. The government should also provide the expenses of works related to Communitisation. The government also needs to carry out its side of the bargain by training the community.

What is School Management Committee? What is the role of SMC vis-a-vis VEC?

In India, a School Management Committee (SMC) is a group established under the Right to Education (RTE) Act, 2009, for every government-run and aided school. The SMC includes parents, teachers, local authorities, and community members. Its primary role is to monitor the school's functioning, prepare the school development plan, and ensure the implementation of the RTE Act, particularly in promoting quality education and addressing issues like student enrollment and retention.

SMCs are provided in the RTE Act while VECs are provided for under Communitisation. Under Communitisation, the VEC oversees over all the schools in the village whereas each school has an SMC. However, since funds for each school are credited to the School Management Development Committee (SMDC), a subsidiary under SMC, the SMCs are more empowered, leading to clashes between SMCs and VECs in certain instances.

What is social capital? Is it relevant to Communitisation?

An easy way to picture social capital is a person who has worked for many years in a large government department making many friends and establishing varied networks among colleagues. A fresh entrant will enjoy less rapport. If the two sets up a business, the person with more networks has a decided advantage. This is an example of social capital capital at work.

Social capital is nothing but the networks, relationships, and norms that enable individuals and groups to work together more effectively to achieve common goals.

Social capital and Communitisation go hand in hand. The idea behind Communitisation is to tap the bond and social cohesion of Naga villages and use it to transform government service delivery system.

What is the connection between Village Development Boards or Village Councils and Communitisation?

The different bodies set up under Communitisation Act works under the supervision of the Village Development Boards and Village Councils.

> *Which has been more successful - VDBs or communitised bodies and why?*

VDBs have proven more successful than communitised bodies due to their dedicated funding and seamless integration into the government administrative system. Additionally, VDBs resonate more with the people, as they are seen as a modern adaptation of the traditional village republics.

> *Do you see any fundamental problem with Communitisation as a governance model?*

In development literature, the need to strengthen grassroots communities has been emphasised. To that extent, Communitisation is a start. However, Communitisation is a case of patching a wound with a Band-Aid. As per the concept of Communitisation, the ownership of government institutions has been transferred to the community. What does that even mean? The village community has been tasked with the job of being inspectors without any modality for reporting or power to correct. Governance is a very specialised function for which we have the bureaucracy.

4

Consensus

How would you answer?

Often, there are voices raised in certain quarters on how the democratic system of voting for decision-making and choosing leaders is alien to the Nagas and that we should go back to consensus-decision making. What is your view on such a call? Can we still go back?

Democratic form of government where decisions are taken through voting is alien to the Nagas. An anthropologist working in Nagaland wrote in a research paper about a graffiti he saw "Election is an insult of each other by vote." What do you say to such a view? Can we abandon democracy?

Discussion

Consensus decision-making served as the most important route of taking decisions in Naga society in the past.

Consensus can be understood as a general agreement or collective opinion reached by a group of people. It involves the process of discussion and negotiation to ensure that all members of the group support or at least accept the final decision or opinion.

Consensus is often used in decision-making processes where agreement is sought among diverse stakeholders to achieve a unified stance or solution.

In public platforms, consensus in decision-making in Nagaland is praised. There are even views in public forums characterising democratic system of voting as alien to the Nagas and that Nagas need to go back to consensus decision-making.

Consensus is arrived at through deliberations and discussions involving all stakeholders. This process considers all opposing voices. A person's perspective may not be included in the final decision but the mere fact of the person expressing it is acknowledged. The decision arrived at reflects the collective will of the community. Since all voices were heard, murmurs and complains on the issue are to be kept to oneself. A person with dignity and honour is not to raise them again. Doing it so would be interpreted as petty. All these involve a lengthy process.

Decisions taken through consensus are not done through voting. The practice of consensus-building in Naga polity is often contrasted with arriving at a decision through voting in a democracy where the principle of "one man, one vote" is practised. Voting, at times, have been condemned as divisive and humiliating for the losing party.

Consensus as a practice of a by-gone era

For consensus to work, it can be argued that, at the least, the following two conditions have to be met:
1. All parties involved should be bound by values of honesty, honour and sacrifice for the common good.
2. No major financial incentive should be in place to be gained.

On the first point, if the disagreeing party is seen as dishonest, without honour, and out there for selfish gains, people refuse to accede to their view or their leadership. In tight-knit Naga communities, where principles of honour played a huge role, leadership positions were not fought over but bestowed by the people. Even now, people go at length to praise the opponent in election rallies. Personally attacking the other person is a case of hitting below the belt for a Naga. If disagreements arise, through a display of goodwill, the parties compete to concede to the other side. The common good is the spirit that moves consensus.

Unfortunately, the concept of consensus in Nagaland has become increasingly difficult to achieve in many areas. The values that once formed the foundation of consensus—honesty, honour, and sacrifice for the common good—were more characteristic of a simpler age, where there were fewer financial incentives to gain from political decisions. In today's world, where financial and economic interests often drive decision-making, rational self-interest tends to prevail. When significant financial stakes are involved, people are naturally inclined to compete rather than cooperate. Altruism works best when there is a sense of reciprocity or when the incentives for personal gain are minimal.

In a certain Chakhesang Naga village, there were two candidates contesting for a seat in the Nagaland Legislative Assembly elections. The villagers met several times to arrive at a "consensus candidate." The deliberations could not produce that candidate. A political agent present at the meetings told the author "Everyone wanted the consensus candidate to be their candidate."

Consensus-decision to consensus-building: reviving the practise of listening to each other

While arriving at consensus decisions are now difficult, a good practice of consensus building was listening to each other, many times resulting in having to listen to old people tell all kind of seemingly non-relevant stories. The old people in the gathering see the need to educate the younger generation on issues confronting them before taking the decision. Consensus-decisions are now futile on many issues but the age-old practice of listening to the other point of view can never go out of fashion, especially as politics become more divisive.

MODEL ANSWERS

Often, there are voices raised in certain quarters on how the democratic system of voting for decision-making and choosing leaders is alien to the Nagas and that we should go back to consensus-decision making. What is your view on such a call? Can we still go back?

The beauty of consensus is that it takes into account all opposing voices. The emphasis of consensus is on the common good and listening to the other person. The concept and practice of consensus is still relevant in that when there are coalition governments, both the opposing parties have to listen to each other and make concessions. However, consensus cannot be the only mode of decision-making because at present there are often heavy financial considerations. Our society is rapidly transitioning from a community-oriented society with all its ethos to a more modern capitalist individualistic society. The old values have their place but we should not impose them on the new. If anything, the spirit of listening to each other and the concern for the common good need to find a place but consensus cannot be the primary mode of decision making. There will be times when all other forms of decision making - voting, bidding, arbitrage, court-ruling, negotiation etc. have to be explored.

Democratic form of government where decisions are taken through voting is alien to the Nagas. An anthropologist working in Nagaland wrote in a research paper about a graffiti he saw "Election is an insult of each other by vote." What do you say to such a view? Can we abandon democracy?

It was Winston Churchill who said "Democracy is the worst form of government except for all other forms of government." It is easy to find fault with democracy but the alternatives are often far worse. Besides, an appreciation of the working of liberal democracy can emerge among Nagas. Majority of Nagas are Christians; the philosophical underpinning of liberal democracy, with its emphasis on individual rights, first emerged as a result of the influence of the Biblical concept 'Man created in the image of God'.

5

Nagaland Liquor Prohibition Act (NLTP Act), 1989

How would you answer?

What are the details of Nagaland Liquor Prohibition Act?

What are the merits of Nagaland Liquor Prohibition Act?

What are the demerits of Nagaland Liquor Prohibition Act?

What does the Bible say on drinking wine? Is the church right in opposing the lifting of Nagaland Liquor Prohibition Act?

Despite the evident fact that the Nagaland Liquor Prohibition Act is not working, why does the church insist on supporting the act?

Agree with the statement: "If it works, alcohol prohibition is a good act".

Disagree with the statement "If it works, alcohol prohibition is a good act".

If I drink a pint of alcohol before retiring to bed, and nothing more, is it still a vice?

If you are an administrator, what will you do regarding NLTP Act?

Discussion

Nagaland Liquor Prohibition Act is an issue the general public agrees is not working but the church leaders are not willing to cede space for its removal. The demerits of the act have been discussed ad nauseam.

Details of Nagaland Liquor Prohibition Act (Important details)

1. Brewing local brew for personal consumption is not prohibited.
2. Brewing local brew for commercial purpose is prohibited.
3. Possession, sale, and brewing of alcohol is prohibited. Emphasise here that even 'possession' of alcohol is prohibited.
4. Punishment: Six months imprisonment for first offence, nine months imprisonment for second offence, twelve months imprisonment for third offence.
5. Exceptions provided in the act: medical prescription from a licensed doctor, and military personnel.

Demerits of Nagaland Liquor Prohibition Act

Loss of revenue to the state government: Prohibition leads to revenue loss to the state government made more precarious by the state government's revenue dependence on the central government and state's persistent budget deficits and high public debt. Since the implementation of GST, there are three major revenue sources for the state government. These are: tax on fuel like diesel and petrol, tax on production and sale of liquor, and property tax. In December 2023, the Manipur government abandoned its policy on prohibition. In doing so, it has provided an annual revenue projection of Rs 600 crore from sale of alcohol in the state[22]. While Manipur's population is higher than Nagaland as per 2011 census with population figures of 26 lakhs for the former and around 20 lakhs for the latter, Manipur's per capita income is lower at around Rs. 95 thousand per annum while Nagaland's per capita income stands at around Rs 1.38 lakhs. Nagaland can expect similar revenue from sale of alcohol.

Not working as alcohol is freely available: The act is not working, evident from the fact that alcohol is freely available throughout the state.

Spurious liquor: NLTP Act has also been blamed for increased consumption of spurious liquor.

Breeds a culture of corruption through bribery to government officials: The act has continued a culture of bribery where government officials and law enforcement bodies have to be bribed for transport and sale of liquor. This breeds a culture of corruption.

Issues of addiction are not highlighted: There is total silence in public discourse on issues of alcohol addiction. Since the society is living the lie of being a "Dry State", a public discourse on ways to help addicts have not taken place. More importantly, government policy and budgetary support on the same is missing.

The church as an institution has an attitude of condemning the act of drinking. The church, by condemning drinking, is handicapped to deal with cases of alcoholism. A caring pastor may pay some home-visits to pray and provide counselling to alcohol

---

[22] Jimmy Leivon, "End to 30 years' liquor sale ban, Manipur to set up beverage cooperation", *The Indian Express*, December 16, 2023, https://indianexpress.com/article/india/end-30-years-liquor-sale-ban-manipur-beverage-cooperation-9071015/

addicts but coming out of addiction require much more than a yearly visit by a pastor. The pastor most often doesn't have the budgetary support nor the training to deal with cases of addiction.

"Prayer centres" have emerged to deal with alcoholics but these are periphery to the church. In fact, outlandish claims under the guise of prophecies or dreams often made in prayer centres have made many prayer centres antagonistic to the church proper. The church is seen as possessing the Biblical authority with all its philosophical foundation and traditions backing it while prayer centres lack them.

Biblical position on drinking

Contrary to popular belief, the Bible does not condemn usage of wine. However, it does condemn drunkenness.

Separation of the church and state

The term 'separation of the church and state' is often used carelessly especially by those in favour of lifting Prohibition. The idea is that the church should not interfere in the governance function of the state. Historical instances of the church's abuse of its authority in governance matter is often cited. The argument is disingenuous for several reasons:

The church doesn't possess the kind of authority ascribed to it anymore. It is true that the emergence of the first states have occurred at the same time organised religion emerged. Religion or appeal to a higher divine authority sanctioned governmental authority. In other words, in order to rule, to say you have been ordained by God gave you legitimacy. This is however, no longer the case. In the Pilgrim's Progress, John Bunyan compared the authority of the Pope to that of a weak old man who could no longer assert his authority. One can replace the Pope in the imagery with the current church and it will work fine. In the imagery, the old Pope was cursing along as the protagonist, Christian, walked by. The church in the capacity of a civil society or a pressure group can pressure the government to do its bidding but beyond that it can do nothing. It is unfortunate that the Nagaland Government has held itself to ransom through the Nagaland Baptist Church Council.

Merits of NLTP Act

Moral stand taken against alcohol addiction since alcohol addiction destroys a lot of families: In fact, the origins of the act can be traced to domestic abuse and poverty caused to families as a result of addiction to alcohol.

Harms of alcohol are made clear: As part of discourse to defend prohibition, the harms of alcohol addictions are made clear to the people.

There are no open bars in Nagaland: Another advantage of NLTP Act is the absence of open bars in Nagaland.

MODEL ANSWERS

Agree with the statement: "If it works, alcohol prohibition is a good act".

Firstly, one has to clarify that the action of drinking itself is not wrong. However, if there is one activity which is prone to abuse and overuse, it is alcohol. Prohibition working perfectly means alcohol is totally absent in the state. What this means is no more domestic violence and dysfunction in the family on account of alcohol, no over-speeding and accidents due to alcoholism, no case of early deaths of bread winners due to substance use. Indeed, if it works, alcohol prohibition is a good act.

Disagree with the statement "If it works, alcohol prohibition is a good act".

The statement comes with it the connotation that drinking alcohol in itself is wrong. It applies a moral yard stick to an action of eating and drinking. Unless liquor has interfered repeatedly in the way of a person's health, work, finances and relationships, I wouldn't condemn it as morally wrong. Also, Nagas have had a long culture of consuming wine as a recreational drink. The act if work perfectly would remove this completely and I would hesitate to eradicate a cultural practice unless it is manifestly wrong.

Follow up Question/Discussion

"My brother died as a result of alcohol addiction. If Prohibition had worked, he would still be alive"

I am very sorry to hear about your personal tragedy. I wish proper help was available so that the tragedy could be averted. Having said so, we are discussing policy decisions when it comes to Prohibition and we have to keep our personal opinions and experiences in their proper place. As a society, proper institutional mechanisms - whether governmental, NGOs, hospitals or welfare groups - have to be in place. Such robust mechanisms when in place would be able to deal with each individual more comprehensively. What we have now is a case of sweeping the issue under the carpet.

"If I drink a pint of alcohol before retiring to bed, and nothing more, is it still a vice?"

Drinking a pint of alcohol before retiring to bed assumes that the alcohol doesn't come in the way of the man's works, his finances and his relationships. Whether that should be labelled a vice or not should be left to the discretion of the individual concerned. Eating too much could be a vice. Not exercising regularly could be a vice.

Procrastination could be a vice. I am not here to arrogate myself to be the judge of a man's character.

If you are an administrator, what will you do?

Any change to the status quo will be a huge issue. I would wait on the consensus to emerge before carrying out any course of action.

6

Youth Unemployment in Nagaland

How would you answer?

Is there really unemployment in Nagaland? Or should there be unemployment in Nagaland? If there is unemployment in Nagaland why do we see many non-locals gainfully employed in different fields? Do not forget they earn high wages!

Why do certain leaders and intellectuals think that unemployment should not be a problem in Nagaland? Do you agree that unemployment should not be a problem in Nagaland?

What are some reasons for unemployment in Nagaland?

What type of unemployment is most prevalent in Nagaland?

What measures would you suggest to solve unemployment problem in Nagaland?

Discussion

Unemployment is an issue countries across the world are facing and any attempt at dismissing the problem should be questioned. This is because, to many, the problem of unemployment in Nagaland is a non-issue. There are people (even public leaders) who genuinely believe that Nagas only have to work harder and reclaim the dignity of labour following which educated youth unemployment would disappear. The most cited example is the presence of non-Nagas throughout Nagaland engaged in

1. Construction sector
2. Owning Shops in the neighbourhood
3. Serving as labourer

On the first, there are approximately 6 lakh youth in Nagaland according to the 2011 census. Whether the construction sector in Nagaland is large enough to absorb all the unemployed youth is questionable. However, not only is being unemployed in the construction sector a matter of willingness of Naga youth, it is also a matter of Naga employers refusing to employ Nagas on their professionalism and productivity.

On the second, social capital and human capital explains the advantage enjoyed by non-Nagas to an extent. Social capital is the advantage that accrues to individuals or groups from their networks of relationships, through which they can access resources, support, or influence. Human capital is the investment a person has made in himself or others so that the person becomes more productive. One of these forms of investment include migration. Non-Nagas enjoy certain advantages as they have better connections with wholesalers (i.e. they enjoy greater Social Capital) and also a better ability to tame the ups and downs of the market through years of perfecting their crafts (through possession of Human Capital).

Unemployment most prominent in Nagaland

In the Economics literature, five types of unemployment are usually identified. These are:

Frictional Unemployment understood as temporary unemployment that occurs when people are transitioning between jobs or entering the workforce for the first time. **Structural Unemployment** or unemployment resulting from a mismatch between workers' skills and the needs of employers, often due to technological changes or shifts in the economy. **Cyclical Unemployment:** Unemployment that occurs due to economic downturns or recessions when overall demand for goods and services decreases. **Seasonal Unemployment:** Unemployment that happens during certain times of the year when demand for specific jobs is lower, such as in agriculture or tourism or construction. **Disguised unemployment**: A situation where more people are employed than are actually needed for a given task or job, leading to a situation where not all workers are fully productive. This type of unemployment is often seen in developing economies or in sectors where labor is abundant but underutilised.

Of these five, **disguised unemployment** has traditionally been understood as the most prevalent type of unemployment in Nagaland. This is because of the high proportion of workers found in the agricultural sector in Nagaland with low contribution to the state's GSDP. An ignored area on discussions of disguised unemployment is the government sector where it can be argued that there is an excess of government employees in the state in many departments.

In recent years, structural unemployment in Nagaland has become as ubiquitous as disguised unemployment. 'Unemployable graduates' or 'graduates without job skills' are terms one sees often.

This problem has been blamed on the education system of the country where the criticism has been on a system that create graduates better employed as clerks – a legacy of the colonial education system. The New Education Policy, 2020 seeks to fix this by placing more importance on skills and employability. To help graduates develop skills, emphasis is being placed on internships and apprenticeships. A model of internships, however, presupposes the existence of formal establishments whether in the service sector or the manufacturing sector. Given the shortage of such institutions in Nagaland, the state is likely to continue falling behind in providing valuable opportunities for skill development and economic growth.

Reasons for Unemployments in Nagaland

Low Skills: Many workers in Nagaland face challenges due to inadequate skills and limited access to training and education, leading to a mismatch between available jobs and the skills of the workforce.

Poor Infrastructure: Nagaland suffers from insufficient infrastructure, including unreliable power supply, inadequate transportation networks, and weak internet connectivity, which hinders economic activities and job creation.

Lack of Private Investment: Capital in Nagaland has been wasted on 'investment' in land in areas around Dimapur district. Investment in land is not productive in that it is not used for production of goods and services. Land is being bought with the expectation that prices would increase, taking the form of speculative asset.

Lack of access to Capital at low interest: Entrepreneurs and small businesses in Nagaland often struggle to access the necessary capital to start or expand their ventures, impeding economic growth and job creation. The unofficial standard rate of interest from money lenders is 5% per month or 60% per annum. This is 300-400% higher than that charged by banks. Lack of access to capital in Nagaland is one big hindrance to development in the state.

Over-Reliance on Government Jobs: There is a heavy dependence on government employment, with many individuals seeking secure jobs in the public sector rather than exploring opportunities in the private sector or entrepreneurship.

Naga Political Problem: The presence of insurgent groups in the state creates instability, raises cost of raw materials, creates fear psychosis and harassment, and discourage investment, further exacerbating unemployment issues.

Low Income: The general income levels in Nagaland are relatively low, affecting consumer spending and limiting economic growth potential, which in turn impacts job availability.

Ways to solve unemployment problem in Nagaland

Improving Infrastructure: Develop and upgrade transportation networks, including roads and railways, to facilitate easier movement of goods and people.

Upgrade Utilities: Ensure a reliable power supply and improve internet connectivity to support businesses and attract investment.

Solving the Naga Political Problem: As long as there are guns tottering around in Nagaland, extortion demands and fear psychosis will discourage investments in Nagaland. Solving Naga political problem is a prerequisite for economic development, and by extension, solving unemployment problem. There is also an unexpressed fear among the general public, revealed only in private conversations, that solving Naga political problem will lead to decreased funding from the central government. Another fear expressed in private conversations is but for the different political groups, the central government would come heavily on the state and take away the rights of the people. Many see the different underground groups as a bargaining chip. As long as these fears of people remain, economic development cannot reach its full potential. There is still a deep mistrust between the common populace and Delhi.

Reviving the Age-Old Dignity of Labour: Every Naga was once engaged in manual labor as a farmer. The call to revive the dignity of labor is a call to embrace various forms of manual work. As incomes have increased and living standards have gone up, many employment opportunities shifted to non-Nagas. For instance, tasks in the construction sector— brickwork, plastering, plumbing, and electrical work— are predominantly carried out by non-locals. In recent years, with rising disposable incomes, new opportunities have emerged, including roles in fixing air conditioners, water purifiers, installing fans, setting up internet cables, etc. Despite these jobs offering good pay, they are often performed by non-locals. The call to dignity of labor is thus an appeal to Naga youth to take on and excel in these works, embracing manual labor as a valuable and respected occupation.

Exploring New Areas of Employment Generation: New areas of employment in Nagaland include emerging sectors such as tourism, agro-processing, and information technology. With its rich cultural heritage and natural beauty, the state has untapped potential in eco-tourism and adventure tourism, which can create jobs in hospitality, guiding, and local crafts. Additionally, promoting agro-processing industries would add value to the state's agricultural products, boosting employment in both rural and urban areas. Further, investment in digital infrastructure can enable growth in the IT and e-commerce sectors, offering opportunities for tech-based services, remote work, and entrepreneurship, thereby diversifying the state's employment landscape.

Model Answers

> *Is there really unemployment in Nagaland? Or should there really be unemployment in Nagaland? Or If there is unemployment in Nagaland why do we see many non-locals gainfully employed in different fields? Do not forget the fact that they earn high wages!*

No society or economy is immune from unemployment problem. The presence of many non-locals in Nagaland in construction, running neighbourhood shops and serving as labourers have given the impression that unemployment shouldn't be a problem in the state. However, whether these three occupations can absorb the mass of unemployed in Nagaland is questionable. More importantly, the state should be more focussed about creating employment which will be as equally lucrative to the high-paying government jobs. This is the area the state is failing miserably. For creating those jobs, an ecosystem that supports entrepreneurship and private investment has to exist and that ecosystem does not exist at present.

> *Why do certain leaders and intellectuals think that unemployment should not be a problem in Nagaland? Do you agree that unemployment should not be a problem in Nagaland?*

Nagaland has one of the highest government employee to total population ratio among all the states in India. 1.25 lakhs on the payroll of the government for approximately 20 lakhs population give a ratio of one government employee for every 16 people in the state. Getting a government job is fairly easy in the state compared to other states. Government jobs pay well creating an ecosystem where providing services for the government employees can create its own circular economy providing numerous opportunities in areas such as construction, driving, education etc. This backward linkage jobs are mostly done by non-locals giving the attitude that if these works are carried out by Naga youth, there would be no unemployment.

The whole world is facing the problem of unemployment. Even if all the backward linkage jobs are taken by Nagas, there will still be unemployment for several reasons, including the rising aspirations and progressing skill sets of Naga youth.

What are some reasons for unemployment in Nagaland?

There are several reasons for unemployment in Nagaland but our unresolved political problem creates a fear psychosis for attracting investment to the state. Added to this is our education system which places more importance on rote learning rather than skills creating a skill-gap. Poor infrastructure increases costs of production.

What type of unemployment is most prevalent in Nagaland?

The majority of our workforce is engaged in agriculture while contributing a minuscule percentage to the state's GSDP. Disguised unemployment is the most prevalent form of unemployment in the state. However, structural unemployment is as serious an issue since many young Nagas are quitting agriculture.

What measures would you suggest to solve unemployment problem in Nagaland?

Upgrading our infrastructure and improving our service delivery will go a long way in reducing cost of business. Dignity of labour and treating all employments with equal respect should be taught in schools. It will be difficult to attract good investments from outside Nagaland as long as Naga political issue is unresolved.

7

Corruption

How would you answer?

Nagas were famous for their honesty. Why then is corruption a big issue in governance in Nagaland?

What steps would you recommend to curb corruption in Nagaland?

The initial reaction of a victim of a crime is often to report it to their community rather than to the police. Could this tendency be attributed to a lack of trust in law enforcement due to corruption?

Discussion

Corruption is typically defined as the abuse of power or authority for personal gain or advantage. It involves actions such as bribery, embezzlement, nepotism, and fraud, where individuals or institutions exploit their positions to benefit themselves or their associates at the expense of fairness, integrity, or public interest.

Government institutions in Nagaland often do not function as mandated, and many of these issues are often labeled corruption. However, many of these stems from the inefficiency of government institutions rather than individual malfeasance. There are many cases where problems arise not because officials are corrupt, but because they either lack the authority to implement policies or their authority is not recognized by the people.

In sociology, Max Weber classifies authority into three types: **Traditional Authority** or authority based on established customs and longstanding practices. This type of authority is often found in monarchies or tribal societies where power is inherited and legitimacy comes from tradition. **Charismatic Authority** or authority based on the personal charm or charisma of an individual leader. The leader's authority comes from their ability to inspire and attract followers, such as revolutionary leaders or influential religious figures. **Legal-Rational Authority** or authority based on formal rules and laws applied systematically and impersonally. This form of authority is typical in modern bureaucracies and democratic institutions, where authority is tied to positions within an organization rather than to individuals personally.

Legal-rational authority is still weak in Nagaland. The younger generation often interprets the lack of legal-rational authority as corruption. This misinterpretation complicates our understanding, as every shortcoming of the state is labeled corruption. However, issues such as insufficient funding, slow project implementation due to bureaucratic hurdles (as opposed to deliberate delays for bribes), and conflicts arising from various ownership systems are not corruption per se, but rather systemic weaknesses that require different solutions.

The state's legal-rational authority in Nagaland is relatively recent and given the communitarian nature of Naga society, the community—whether in the form of a clan, village, or tribe—can effectively challenge state authority. The presence of multiple actors within the society means that community pressure alone does not constitute corruption. However, when individuals within the government manipulate rules and practices to favour community interests at the expense of others, it crosses into the realm of corruption. The influence of the Naga political movement is significant; underground leaders can coerce government officials into granting funds and jobs. This coercion becomes corruption when officials yield to these demands. Needless to say, low state capacity coupled with corruption has made Nagaland's government very inefficient.

Different Forms of Corruption in Nagaland

Corruption manifests differently depending on the perspective of the observer. An ordinary person might view corruption as a high-ranking official embezzling funds for personal gain. A government official, on the other hand, might see it as a village community manipulating census data to secure more funding. An anthropological understanding of corruption highlights these varying perspectives and is used to examine different cases within the state.

Accepting Money During Elections: One of the most cited forms of corruption in Nagaland is the practice of giving and receiving money during elections. Candidates often spend vast amounts of money to secure victory, making it nearly impossible for honest candidates who do not distribute funds to win. This financial pressure leads to further corruption as candidates seek to recoup their expenses. Women candidates facing significant challenges in winning elections is a consequence of this practice. Despite efforts by the Election Commission of India and the Nagaland Baptist Church Council, this practice remains pervasive.

Proxy Voting: Proxy voting involves individuals voting on behalf of non-existent or absent voters. On election day, genuine voters cast their votes first, and once they finish voting, votes are cast for those not present or even deceased. The Election Commission of India and the state administration are working to address this issue. Additionally, substitute voting, where one person votes for their entire family, is illegal but still commonly occurs.

Providing Exaggerated Data: A notable form of corruption is the manipulation of data to gain advantages. Villages in Nagaland increasing their population count to gain advantage during elections is an open secret. Another reason for providing exaggerated data is to gain more funds. There is also competitive pride among different communities to have government institutions or higher government authorities in their place. Thus, one come across people say "Our town was founded first but it has only an EAC whereas they have an ADC HQ though the town was formed after us." Or "If we count our households and population properly, we are no less than them but in the census theirs is higher than ours; they are able to do well in elections accordingly." Or "Our leaders are not united; we should have an SDO office by now." This competitive behavior, similar to the "race to the bottom" seen in competitions to lower taxation and environmental regulations, wastes resources, creates a distorted picture of local needs and priorities.

Different Cuts by Ministers and Administrative Heads on Contracts: In Nagaland, a pernicious form of corruption is deducting a certain percentage from funds released for government projects and contracts as bribes by elected officials and administrative heads. The practice has become so wretched to the point even beneficiaries of funds released through direct benefit transfers (DBT) have to pay a certain percentage to the authorities who released the funds. To the Nagas, government exist merely to allocate resources, the other side of the government receiving funds through taxation from the people is still missing, and as such though people complain the outrage is absent.

Giving Jobs to Kins and Party Workers: Nepotism is prevalent when government positions, are given to family members or party supporters. This undermines meritocracy and professionalism in the public sector. This practice, however, has been curtailed to an extent through direct recruitments from NPSC and NSSB in recent years.

Essential Insights 7.1 Theory of Kin Selection and Inclusive Fitness

According to the theory of Kin Selection and Inclusive Fitness proposed by evolutionary biologist William D. Hamilton, "altruistic behavior is proportional to shared genes." Hamilton explained that individuals are more likely to act altruistically toward close relatives because it increases the chances of their shared genes being passed to future generations. Relatives share a portion of their genes due to common ancestry; for example, siblings share approximately 50% of their genes, so helping a sibling supports the survival of shared genetic material.

Hamilton's Rule formalizes this idea, stating that altruistic behavior is favored when the cost to the individual is outweighed by the benefit to the relative, adjusted for their genetic relatedness. This principle helps explain why individuals prioritize supporting their kin. In real-life examples, it appears as behaviors such as parents sacrificing for their children or siblings helping and cooperating with each other. It also accounts for nepotism and corruption, where individuals may favor family members at the expense of fairness or ethical standards. This evolutionary perspective reveals that altruistic behavior is not simply an act of kindness but a strategy for enhancing genetic survival.

Neglecting Jobs: Problem of Dereliction of Duty: Poor infrastructure and lack of proper accommodation for government employees in many parts of Nagaland lead to absenteeism. Many employees use these conditions as excuses for not attending work. This situation results in disguised unemployment and a general lack of professionalism within government offices.

Pilferage of Rations: The pilferage of government rations is another issue, where supplies intended for public distribution are siphoned off for personal gain. This form of corruption deprives the intended recipients of essential resources.

Providing Permits or Licenses Without Due Diligence: Government officials often sign building permits or provide licenses without proper scrutiny, driven by a belief that regulations are cumbersome. This practice, while simplifying processes for some, can lead to significant problems, such as traffic congestion and poorly constructed infrastructure. This is a common practice in the Transport Department where vehicles purchased outside Nagaland often seek registration in Nagaland through bribes, where, ironically, strict enforcement would lead to public backlash. The ease of registration contributes to traffic congestion and other related problems.

Police and Law Enforcement: In many cases, manipulating FIRs by police in Nagaland reflects a form of corruption where cases are deliberately altered, delayed, or dismissed to protect influential individuals. This undermines justice, erodes public trust in law enforcement, and perpetuates a culture of impunity.

Education: Issues such as absentee teachers, improper recruitment, and transfers hamper the functioning of government schools. The public perceives these issues as abuses of authority, contributing to dissatisfaction and corruption.

Pensions and GPF: Obtaining pensions or accessing General Provident Fund (GPF) benefits often requires bribes, causing delays and dissatisfaction among retirees. Government employees periodically withdraw their GPF amount so as not to accumulate large amounts to prevent paying higher amount of bribes. Since the state government's finance is dire with the need for constant resource mobilisation through debt financing, bribery serve indirectly as dent on the state's exchequer.

Reasons for Corruption in Nagaland

There are primarily three reasons for corruption in Nagaland:

Corruption Due to Social Pressure to Maintain Communitarian Ethos

It has reduced to a significant extent, but leaders are expected to channel resources from the government to benefit their community members, including family and tribe. A leader who can distribute resources is considered generous, while one who adhered strictly to the law without such distribution is viewed as selfish. This expectation has created a system of corruption where leaders are pressured to provide material benefits to their communities, often through means that involves bending or breaking the rules.

This phenomenon is akin to what has been observed in other regions. For instance, in Papua New Guinea, when government institutions were first introduced as in Nagaland, tribal leaders focused on extracting resources from the government for their tribes rather than advancing the broader national interest, a phenomenon sometimes referred to as "big-man" politics. Similarly, in Greece, members of different governments appointed their own family members to public institutions. Since government employees were usually difficult to replace, the number of public sector workers kept increasing. As a result, the wage bill grew, and the government had to borrow money to cover it. This contributed to the Greece debt crisis, which began around 2009. In Nagaland, the pressure to meet communal expectations often leads to corruption, as leaders navigate between their official duties and the demands of their communities.

Corruption Due to a Weak Government or Low State Capacity

Corruption in Nagaland is facilitated by a weak state structure and low state capacity. There is no fear of being caught and penalised even when abusing the given mandated authority. Nagaland was formed as a pacifier or compromise from full demand for sovereignty. The central government has been unwilling or uninterested to exert its power in demanding transparency for funds it released. Historically, the Government of Nagaland also prefers to be on the good books of the central government by often siding with it politically in the parliament.

The Naga political groups are also able to effectively challenge the authority of the state, facilitating corruption.

Corruption Due to Personal Greed and Thirst for Power

Corruption also arises from a person's desire to be recognised, get rich and be influential. It is the job of government regulatory, law enforcement, court and audit institutions to keep the personal vices in check. In a state where these institutions are weak, room for expressing personal vices grow, allowing corruption to flourish unchecked.

Ways to Tackle Corruption in Nagaland

Strengthening Accountability Mechanisms: Establish independent anti-corruption bodies with the authority to investigate and prosecute corruption cases without political interference. As a start, **Strengthen the Nagaland Lokayukta:** The Lokayukta officers currently lack the power to arrest and do not benefit from custodial interrogation or the ability to register criminal cases. Since the enactment of the Act in 2017, no FIR has been lodged due to the absence of a police station and an officer in charge[23]. The following suggestions are available in public to address these issues:

1. Designating the director of the Nagaland Lokayukta as a police station and appointing the director as the officer in charge.
2. Clearly defining the powers and jurisdiction of the Nagaland Lokayukta police.
3. Establishing a special court under Section 3(1) of the Prevention of Corruption Act to enhance the Lokayukta's effectiveness in tackling corruption.

Enhancing Transparency in Government Transactions: Implement digital platforms for public access to government contracts, budgets, and expenditures to promote transparency and discourage corrupt practices.

Promoting Citizen Participation: Encourage active involvement of civil society organizations and community groups in monitoring government projects and expenditures, fostering a culture of accountability.

Whistleblower Protection: Enact and enforce strong laws to protect whistleblowers who report corruption, ensuring they are safeguarded against retaliation.

Regular Training and Capacity Building: Provide ongoing training for government officials on ethical practices, integrity, and the

---

[23] Correspondent, "Proposal to Empower Nagaland Lokayukta," Nagaland Post, June 4, 2023, https://nagalandpost.com/index.php/2023/06/04/proposal-to-empower-nagaland-lokayukta/

importance of transparency to instill a culture of accountability within public service.

Model Answers

Nagas were famous for their honesty. Why then is corruption a big issue in governance in Nagaland?

For many years, the state's authority was weak due to the government being a relatively recent modern institution in Nagaland, coupled with the Naga political movement. People who got into governmental positions took it as an opportunity to enrich themselves and their communities since there was little oversight. In fact, people in authority who did not help their community members were seen as corrupt and selfish.

What steps would you recommend to curb corruption in Nagaland?

Many steps by the government such as e-pay, PIMS code, direct benefit transfer, transparent bidding are all steps in the right direction. Corruption in Nagaland is an issue that will require political solutions similar to the rise of AAP in Delhi in 2013, the coming to power of Congress in Karnataka in 2023 and the emergence of Modi in 2014 when they directly raise the issue of corruption as a political issue.

The initial reaction of a victim of a crime is often to report it to their community rather than to the police. Could this tendency be attributed to a lack of trust in law enforcement due to corruption?

The case you mentioned is a case of the people not recognising the state's authority rather than a case of corruption. The police does sometimes practice corruption by changing the seriousness of FIR, refusing to file FIR for fear that registering the FIR and not solving the case may impede future promotions etc. However, reporting to the police might not come instinctively because the state has not consistently demonstrated its capability to deliver justice or provide effective solutions. It should be seen as people's lack of recognition of state's authority rather than corruption per se.

8

Clean election movement

How would you answer?

Why is Clean Election Movement in Nagaland a failure despite the best effort of the NBCC?

Should NBCC continue with the Clean Election Movement?

Discussion

The key question around clean election in Nagaland is why despite the best effort of the NBCC not much progress has been made. It is important to note that the issue of clean election in Nagaland is not limited to persuading voters not to accept money during elections but include preventing other malpractices such as use of alcohol and manipulating the voters' list. The concern raised by NBCC is that a candidate to contest elections have to mobilise resources who then has to resort to corruption to raise those resources. After winning elections, the candidates have to mobilise resources again to recoup what they have spent.

The issue of corruption is thus two-fold:

1.   Mobilising resources to distribute before elections

2.   Mobilising resources to recoup what has been spent

A person who worked closely with a minister told this author, "Often, even ministers are highly in debt after elections, they have to pay 70-80 lakhs as interest every month."

Why Clean Election Movement fails: Argument given in public forums

Clean election movement has failed to deter voters receiving money during elections. The reason attributed to it in public forums is voters' poverty and ignorance. The explanation on poverty is self-explanatory. When a family struggling to make ends meet is offered not an insignificant amount of money to vote for a certain candidate, it is often difficult to refuse that monetary incentive. The church, as an institution, is expected to care for the poor within its fold. However, various factors have constrained its ability to fulfil this role effectively:

a) The proliferation of churches due to numerous denominations and divisions,

b) The church taking on too many projects,

c) The burden of numerous organizations and activities within the church.

A day might arise when people begin questioning whether the church is merely receiving material contributions without giving back in return – the business of making church a business. There are already murmurs on the size of church budgets and physical development that comes at the cost of members' welfare.

The argument that voters are ignorant is disingenuous.

Why voters receive incentive to vote for certain candidates: Naga communitarian ethos

Nagas have a culture of sharing and supporting each other within their social groups. Sharing ones' resources need not always be quid pro quo. A Naga seeking leadership through elections by distributing money reflects the culture of sharing and mutual help in the community. Thus, when goods or money is distributed, it is not given as a pure market exchange of "I pay you money, you give me your vote". In fact, an aspiring candidate tests the water (as it were) by distributing goods to all the households typically to his village or organise a feast for the whole village of his own or even another usually during Christmas. Even when money is distributed to the voters, it is usually done by someone who is close to the voter. A candidate who gives the highest amount of money does not always win. The candidate has to demonstrate his strength and worthiness through his ability to provide for his constituency but the general qualities of being a good person and a good leader through compassion, politeness, public standing and alliance making in villages beyond his own are necessary traits.

In many cultures, accepting gifts is seen as a gesture of fostering friendship. In Nagaland, accepting money during elections partly reflects this cultural tradition. The money symbolizes a commitment to strengthening the bond between the candidate and the voter, signifying their intent to work together. Over the years, the amount of money and resources involved has increased significantly, making it increasingly unaffordable.

Voters receiving incentive to vote: Lesson from other countries

While accepting money by voters during elections is seen as the only reason why the state is poor, it is important to note that other democracies have gone through the same problem.

Firstly, poor people compared to the rich may not have equal stake in the policies and programs of the government. An illustration: The fast pace national highway construction by the central government from 2014-2024 has been much lauded for improving the ease and speed of transport and communication. However, there are also calls that the focus of the government should be on other forms of infrastructure such as foot paths, streetlights, town libraries, proper drainage, etc. where the common populace will benefit more. The argument is that national highways and express ways disproportionately benefit the rich. Another illustration is the case of Vande Bharat trains. If one studies the reason for railway accidents in India, the reason boils down to "too many passengers and trains, too less investments". Investments on railways in India might be better served in upgrading existing projects rather than taking up fast paced green field projects.

Secondly, in a poor state or country (like ours), giving money to the electorate is an incentive to merely take the trouble to go out and vote.

Thirdly, the cost becomes too high for the candidates to afford as the economy grows and the income of the people rises.

Fourthly, governance could become very inefficient that pressure groups themselves begin to rally against incentivising voters. This was the case in USA. During Andrew Jackson's presidency (1829–1837), the "spoils system" became widespread, where political supporters were rewarded with government jobs, often without qualifications. This led to inefficiency and corruption in public administration. Public demand for reform grew, especially after President James Garfield's assassination by a disgruntled office-seeker in 1881. In response, the Pendleton Civil Service Reform Act of 1883 established a merit-based system, improving government efficiency and curbing corruption.

Fifthly, apart from taking care of basic needs of the people, a government has to work to take into account the growing aspirations of the people as income and education of the people grows.

Sixth, related to the fifth point, as income of people grows, the electorates prefer proper functioning of institutions and proper policies.

The income of the people of Nagaland will have to grow significantly before the practice of accepting money during elections is curbed.

Model Answers

Why is Clean Election Movement in Nagaland a failure despite the best effort of the NBCC?

The Clean Election Movement in Nagaland has been a failure because the sharing of one's resources is a part of Naga communitarian ethos seen in practices such as feast of merit, a hunter sharing his game, and the community coming together to help construct a person's house. In fact, taking care of each other is given as an explanation for why Naga society as a whole do not have beggars. Even now, we see the values of sharing coming into full bloom during times of sickness, death, weddings, and supporting members of a community in sports. To many, giving and receiving money during elections is an extension of this culture.

Political scientists have also pointed how for a poor person, the receiving of money is an incentive to merely go out and vote since he or she has very little stake in the day-to-day activities of the government.

Follow-up question:

Are you blaming our culture then? Is there something wrong with our culture?

It is said that we shouldn't judge a philosophy on its abuse. In our case, inducing voters with money is an abuse of our culture of sharing. One cannot blame our culture.

Follow-up question:

Based on your answer, there is no hope then. Since mobilising resources for elections is one of the primary reasons for corruption and poor workmanship in Nagaland, the state will remain forever corrupted?

Other countries have walked the path we have walked. History of democracies show that when the income of a country has risen high enough, it becomes too expensive for the candidates to induce voters to vote for them since the inducements for voters keep getting higher. Also, as the income of voters become higher, they prefer well-functioning institutions over temporary cash or material inducements.

Should NBCC continue with the Clean Election Movement?

Yes. Though the movement has not been successful, the church is the conscience keeper of the state and it has to keep harping on that message. The beauty of the movement is that the Election Commission of India is fully on full board with the NBCC.

9

Land Ownership Issue

How would you answer?

What aspect of land ownership system creates the most problems in Nagaland?

Is land ownership issue as big a problem as it is being make out to be?

Land in regions around Dimapur is being viewed as investment similar to how gold is viewed in mainland India? What facilitates this? Is it productive to invest in land?

What problem does rapidly increasing land prices cause in Nagaland?

Discussion

Land ownership system has been labelled the biggest hurdle impeding development in Nagaland several times by different ministers on separate occasions. The problems faced in Nagaland with regard to purchase, sale, transfer and disposal of land are inherent within the land ownership system and the laws, practices, customs and conventions surrounding it. To a significant extent, the problems that normally arise in Nagaland around land is a result of the dual nature of land:

1. Land is an economic asset
2. The same piece of land possesses deep-rooted socio-cultural importance.

Where land has less socio-cultural relevance, say in a district like Dimapur and the districts surrounding it like Niuland and Chumoukedima, the problems surrounding it has been lower. To understand the issues facing land in Nagaland require a deeper understanding of the land ownership system.

Features of Land Ownership System in Nagaland

1.   Different Entities Hold Land in Nagaland

Different entities hold land in Nagaland. Often, the landholding entities are divided into two: i) private individual or household and ii) community. The government is sometimes added as the third land owning entity. However, this division is too broad and leaves out certain important sub-entities who play equally crucial roles in understanding the land ownership system. The land ownership system can be categorised into the following:

- i.   **Individual/Family/Household** owned by the males
- ii.   **Daughter/Woman**, with the understanding that the plot of land would be returned to one of her brothers after her demise
- iii. **Small extended Family**: common land inherited from father among siblings, with each family having the right to use the plot of land

iv. **Larger extended Family**: inherited from grandfather or great grandfather with everyone having the right to use the plot of land

v. **Clan:** Land is managed by clans, with decisions made by clan leaders usually through consensus. Inheritance follows traditional customs.

vi. **Village**: Land is managed by village councils, with use and inheritance following village customs.

vii. **Government**: Government has come to owned huge tracts of land through acquisition.

In studies on land in Nagaland, land owned by small extended families and larger extended families are ignored. However, most of the problems around purchase and transfer of land occur on account of these types of ownership. Our forefathers did not always see the need to demarcate land separately for each child. Over the years, as population increase and more forest areas are brought under development, when a plot of land is sought to be sold or purchased, trying to identify an owner, in many cases, has become a nightmare.

2. Dominance of unregistered land ownership

There is dual status of land with regard to registration with the existence of both registered and unregistered land ownership systems. However, unregistered land ownership dominates.

3. No definite owner or existence of multiple owners

With multiple landowners, whether the plot of land is owned by small extended family, large extended family, clan or village, the ownership system is very different from ownership of other forms of property in that with the latter, often the owner is easy to identify and locate.

4. **Land ownership and transfer of resources governed by customary laws**

A feature of customary laws is that private property rights are not respected. As such, even if a piece of land legally belongs to a person, occasions will arise where the person cannot sale the land to a person from another village, tribe or a non-Naga.

Almost all the problems on issues surrounding land arise from these four features of land ownership system. Consider certain scenarios:

1. A person in order to buy a plot of land from an individual has to ensure that the plot of land belongs to him alone and not to his extended family or clan. Almost every family in Nagaland is familiar with cases where a person buys a plot of land from an individual only for complications to emerge later that the seller isn't the sole proprietor. The extended families complain vehemently upon discovery that the plot of land has been sold without their knowledge and refuses to give up the plot of land. In many cases, the seller has spent the money and cannot return it. The buyer buys the same plot of land multiple times in order to secure clear ownership and resolve disputes with all parties involved. The buyer not only lose money by buying multiple times but has to bear cost of transactions for gathering information on the plot of land and the seller. This is an instance of problems arising from multiple owners.

2. A person wants to sell a plot of land that legally belongs to him but he cannot find a buyer because the village community has made a resolution that the plot of land cannot be sold to a person from another village. This is an instance of problem arising from customary law. In a district

like Dimapur, land is not constraint by these landownership systems, thus there is often a single individual owning the plot of land, and the person, in most cases, is free to sell it to anyone.

3. Villages around Kohima have excess perennial springs which could be rented out to the capital city for premium prices. The villages refuse to do so driven by a strong sense of ownership and reluctance to relinquish control over their natural resources. The villages have made sub-optimal economic decisions in this instance. The state does not see itself as having enough stake or *locus standi* to mediate and provide water for the capital city.

Suggested solutions on Land Ownership issue in public

Currently, there are limited studies or comprehensive suggestions addressing land issues in Nagaland. A notable suggestion comes from Yanpvuo Kikon, who proposes two potential measures to address these challenges[24]:

1. Cadastral surveys or Mapping of land

2. Land registration

Problems around land ownership arises when there are multiple owners or where no definite owner can be identified. In such cases, even registration will be difficult.

Issues around land demarcation will only get worse. Land is a scarce resource the supply of which do not increase with increasing population.

---

[24] Yanpvuo Kikon, "Understanding the Basic Fundamentals of Land Ownership in the Context of Nagaland," The Morung Express, June 30, 2018.

A painful and uncomfortable conversation around dividing up land and getting it registered is inevitable going forward. As land ownership disputes intensify, particularly with multiple claimants and undefined boundaries, communities will be forced to confront these issues head-on. Dividing ancestral land, which often holds deep emotional and cultural significance, is likely to lead to tensions within families and between neighbouring groups. Furthermore, the process of formalising ownership through registration may challenge long-standing customary practices, creating resistance to change. However, despite the discomfort, this dialogue is essential for ensuring clarity, reducing future disputes, and establishing legal ownership rights, especially as land becomes increasingly scarce with population growth. It may require not only legal reforms but also social and communal adjustments to ensure that the process moves forward constructively and equitably.

MODEL ANSWERS

What aspect of land ownership system creates the most problems in Nagaland?

Land owned by small extended families and large extended families are causing most of the problems in Nagaland. Often, a person buys a plot of land from an individual only for his extended family to complain that the land he bought never belonged exclusively to the seller in the first place.

Is land ownership issue as big a problem as it is being make out to be?

Yes, identifying the land owner can be cumbersome. Also, customary laws can have their own set of demands. People, in many cases, are not ready to have the difficult conversation of having to split up the land and demarcating the boundaries and owners clearly.

Land in regions around Dimapur is being viewed as investment similar to how gold is viewed in mainland India? What facilitates this? Is it productive to invest in land?

Increasing urbanisation is one reason why land prices are rising rapidly in areas around Dimapur. However, urbanisation is only a partial explanation. Land in that district and the regions surrounding it are not bound by strict customary laws, as also the demands to sell only to a customer from a specific tribe or village. Also, land as an asset is more liquid (i.e. more easily convertible to cash) since there are more buyers and sellers. This increases the attractiveness of land as an asset. Locating the actual owner is also easier, as also the ease of documentation.

Land is not a productive investment as it does not directly facilitate production of goods and services. It is a form of speculation. Buying land in areas around Dimapur is also a hedge against inflation.

What problem does rapidly increasing land prices cause in Nagaland?

One reason for rapidly increasing land prices is inequality in access to monetary resources in the state. Rapidly increasing land prices is both a cause and a consequence of rising inequality in Nagaland. The biggest consequence of rapidly increasing land prices is housing problem in urban areas.

What is the SARFAESI Act? Is it applicable in Nagaland?

The SARFAESI Act (Securitization and Reconstruction of Financial Assets and Enforcement of Security Interest Act) of 2002 allows banks and financial institutions in India to recover defaulted loans by selling or repossessing secured assets without court intervention.

The Act enables the securitization of financial assets and the reconstruction of distressed assets, aiming to improve the efficiency of the asset recovery process and reduce non-performing assets (NPAs).

Yes, the act is applicable in Nagaland with modification i.e. the asset is to be transferred only to indigenous population of Nagaland.

10

Non-performing Government Schools in rural areas: a legacy issue of wrong recruitment practices

How would you answer?

> *Despite having the best teachers and infrastructure, why do government schools suffer from low enrolment in Nagaland?*
>
> *What is transfer of teacher with post?*
>
> *Is communitisation of schools in Nagaland a success or failure?*

Discussion

The biggest problem most government schools face at present is low student enrollment. This was not an issue 20 years ago. What happened?

In Nagaland, education has two competing suppliers: private and government. Government schools have lost out to private schools, their competitors. The question then is, since government schools have more qualified teachers with higher pay and remuneration, why do parents prefer private schools? The answer is obvious: private schools demonstrate the proper functioning of institutions by holding regular classes, conducting morning assemblies, organising parents' days, and other literary and co-curricular activities.

The minimal requirement parents had was the proper running of classes. When this was not provided, parents complained and sought reforms, but reforming government schools proved to be extremely difficult.

Firstly, the recruitment of teachers was not done through competitive exams. Many teachers were appointed directly by the education department without the posts being advertised. In fact, teachers would be appointed on contract only to be regularised later on.

Secondly, since teachers preferred to be posted in their native places, where their spouses were located, or in urban areas, a phenomenon called "transfer of teacher along with post" took place in Nagaland. This led to a situation where many government schools in rural areas were without science or math teachers. When "transfer of teacher along with post" was not possible, teachers kept local "substitute teachers" - teachers who would work in their places with the payment of a token amount. Since teaching posts were also transferred in many cases as mentioned above, the much maligned "proxy teachers" became a necessity in many cases.

When people complained, the complains fell on deaf ears. Very importantly, government schoolteachers were among the most educated, and the richest in the village. Teachers were also often public leaders. Thus, even when schools were not functioning, the public could not challenge or put pressure on the teachers.

When attempts at reforming government schools proved futile, highly motivated and respected individuals (mostly within the church) who treated education on a mission mode step in to fill the void of providing quality education. Private school teachers were and are overburdened, are mostly inexperienced and have to work with extreme low pay. However, they take classes the whole allotted day. Enrollment in private schools kept increasing while the opposite happened in government schools.

Enrollment in government schools have now fallen so low that even with the issues mentioned above fixed, students have not enrolled. Low students' enrollment is extremely demotivating for the teachers. Since everyone who can afford it send their children to private schools, only the poorest, the most uneducated and dysfunctional families in the villages send their children to government schools. With such children, learning does not take place at home, thus removing an important component of education. Low enrolment and low-quality students make teaching challenging.

Failing government schools exacerbates inequality. Government schools work better where teachers do not occupy the top hierarchy in the society. In poorer villages and towns, there is no one to oversee their works. In villages where there are many people richer, more educated and whose standing in society is higher than teachers, the community serve as a check from teachers' dereliction of duty. Government schools run properly, proper infrastructure is provided and students demonstrate their learning through good results. Since government schools' fees are minimal to non-existent, given the good quality of schools, the schools attract quality students. A virtuous cycle kicks in. Parents from more developed villages thus do not pay school fees even though they can afford. In less developed villages, parents face difficulty paying the school fees of their children but to ensure quality education, send their children to private schools. This takes away resources meant for higher education, leading to more inequality.

Teachers were recruited from outside Nagaland, especially to teach Math and Science. However, with the completion of their service duration, local teachers have been recruited. A benefit of this change has been the employment of local youth. However, many complain about the deterioration of professionalism compared to recruits from more advanced states.

Biometric attendance

Biometric attendance is often touted as a solution. There is reluctance to adopt this technology from the teachers. The infrastructure that supports the technology is also absent. Power supply in Nagaland is erratic which is worse in rural areas. In many places, smooth internet connection is a luxury.

However, teachers' attendance is not big an issue as it once was. Low enrolment is the bigger problem. Low enrolment is a legacy issue. It will take many years for government schools to demonstrate competence and for parents to put their trust in government schools again.

Despite having the best teachers, infrastructure and almost zero school fees, why do government schools suffer from low enrolment in Nagaland?

Government schools have their own competitors in the form of private schools. Nagaland, as a state, suffers from government institutions whether they are financial, health, law enforcement or education. The central government institutions work better because institutions are more developed. Nagaland is still learning to be on its feet, not only financially but institutionally as well. Government schools in Nagaland suffer the same institutional malaise and weaknesses the other institutions suffer from. While things are being fixed, it is yet to come out of the legacy issues of wrong recruitment, substitute teachers, absentee teachers and proxy teachers. It will take years for perception to change.

What is transfer of teacher with post?

Teachers preferred posting in urban areas. In many cases, they could not receive transfer as someone had to transfer out in their place. It was a zero-sum game. Teachers with strong political backing and support in the departments transferred along with their posts! In many cases, these were Science and Math teachers. Schools in far flung rural areas could not function without those teachers. It contributed to the demise of the government schools in Nagaland.

Is *communitisation of schools in Nagaland a success or failure?*

Communitisation record is mixed. It is very successful in certain areas whereas it is not the case in others. Strangely, communitisation has been successful where schools were successful before whereas they have failed where schools were weak before. On cursory reading, the policy has been more successful in richer and more educated villages whereas they have been less successful in poorer, less literate villages. One explanation for this is that in richer villages, teachers do not hold the top position in societal hierarchy. Teachers can thus be disciplined. In poorer villages, teachers are among the most educated and the richest in the village, often serving as public leaders. It is difficult to discipline them from the perspective of the village community. The government sought to make the community an accountable partner to the government institutions. This has however not been very effective.

11

Inner Line Permit (ILP)

How would you answer?

What is ILP?

Explain the importance of ILP to the Nagas.

Do you think ILP is alienating the Nagas from being integrated properly into the Indian union?

Is ILP fair to outsiders who wants to come to Nagaland?

Discussion

An Inner Line Permit (ILP) is a document that allows Indian citizens to visit or stay in certain protected states in India. This system is currently in place in four Northeastern states: **Arunachal Pradesh, Nagaland, Mizoram and Manipur**. Citizens who are not originally from one of these states cannot visit without an ILP and cannot stay longer than the permit allows.

The ILP system has its origins in the British colonial era. In 1873, the British created rules under the Bengal Eastern Frontier Regulation Act to control who could enter and stay in certain areas, primarily to protect British business interests by preventing Indians (who were then British subjects) from trading in those regions. After India's independence, the term "British subjects" was replaced with "Citizens of India" to protect the interests of the local indigenous people from outsiders belonging to other Indian states.

Today, an ILP is issued by the state government concerned and can be obtained either online or in person. The ILP specifies the travel dates and the particular areas within the state that the holder is allowed to visit.

The arguments for ILP

Protection against influx of Migrants: The case of Tripura

In any discussion on the need for ILP in Nagaland, the most cited example is Tripura. In Tripura, the tribal population during 1941-51 was 47%. The country gained independence, partition took place and as a result of migration into Tripura by Bengali Hindus, the tribal population as a proportion of total population decreased to 29% in 1981 [25]. An unfortunate interplay was the lost of land belonging to tribals which led to violent conflicts later. The fear often expressed is a similar scenario playing out in Nagaland and other states where ILP is in place.

Low Population and Fragile Community Composition

Nagaland has a population of nearly 2 million with a population density of 119 persons per square kilometre as per 2011 census. It is an open secret that census figures are often inflated to gain electoral advantage and as such the population is expected to be much lower. With a small population, the apprehensions often

---

[25] Arunodoy Saha, "Chapter 9: Tripura," in Unspecified Title, The Institute of Developing Economies (IDE), accessed December 3, 2024, https://www.ide.go.jp/library/English/Publish/Reports/Jrp/pdf/133_11.pdf.

expressed is that an influx of outsiders could lead to increased competition for resources, potentially leading to displacement and loss of control over traditional lands. People outside the northeast at times complain against ILP measures since residents from states where ILP is in place can travel and work freely throughout the country. ILP, to them, violates Article 19 of the Indian constitution that grants freedom to reside and settle in any part of the country of India. Understanding the historical and cultural context behind ILP is essential to appreciate its rationale and its role in preserving the identity, resources, and traditions of indigenous communities.

Need for Protection of tribals: Experience in other countries

In other countries, indigenous and tribal communities have faced varying degrees of challenges related to protecting their land, culture, and rights.

North America (United States and Canada): Indigenous tribes in the U.S. and Canada faced extensive land dispossession through treaties, wars, and legislation. Without adequate protection, they lost vast territories, which led to the erosion of their traditional lifestyles and cultures.

Australia: Aboriginal Australians experienced severe land loss due to colonization, and the lack of early protections led to the disruption of their social structures, culture, and economy. The "Stolen Generations" policy, where Aboriginal children were removed from their families, further devastated communities.

Latin America (Brazil, Peru): In countries like Brazil and Peru, indigenous tribes in the Amazon have faced encroachment by loggers, miners, and settlers. This has led to violence, displacement, and environmental degradation. The lack of strong legal protections has left these communities vulnerable.

Africa: Many African tribal communities, like the Maasai in Kenya and Tanzania or the San in Southern Africa, have been marginalized and displaced from their traditional lands due to colonial policies and post-colonial development projects. Without sufficient protections, they have often been forced into poverty and dependency.

Efforts to correct historical wrongs in these countries have seen only limited success, as ongoing struggles with recognition, protection, and autonomy persist despite some legal and policy advancements.

Ineffectiveness of ILP: "ILP only in name"

The Inner Line Permit (ILP) was initially established primarily to protect British colonial interests rather than solely the welfare of indigenous communities. Over time, the rationale evolved to emphasize protecting indigenous tribes from external exploitation. For the locals, the ILP has come to be seen as a protective measure against external exploitation and intrusion, safeguarding their cultural identity and resources. However, the presence of many non-locals provides credence to the argument that ILP protection exist only in name.

The arguments of the ineffectiveness of ILP in protecting tribals can be summarised as:

a) cultural and language homogenisation from increased interactions

b) economic exploitations by outsiders

c) Limited Effectiveness

Cultural Homogenisation: The claim that the ILP protects local languages and cultures is problematic due to homogenisation of languages, developed out of necessity. In Arunachal Pradesh, for example, there are multiple language groups—Tibetan dialect

116

speakers in the west, Tani language speakers in the center, and Tai-related language speakers in the east. Hindi has emerged as a common language due to this diversity. Similarly, in Nagaland and Mizoram, the development of lingua franca like Nagamese and Mizo, respectively, reflects a shift away from smaller tribal languages, challenging the notion that the ILP effectively preserves linguistic diversity. Though it can be argued that this cultural harmonisation of language has occurred not because of but in spite of ILP, the homogenisation highlights the limitations of protective mechanisms in addressing the practical realities of communication and coexistence in diverse linguistic environments.

Economic Exploitation: The argument that the ILP protects tribes from exploitation by outsiders is weakened by the dominance of non-locals in local businesses and construction sector. Developmental projects carried with expertise from outsiders have also caused environmental harms. Hydro-electric projects in Arunachal has caused environmental hazards both in the state and in the downstream state of Assam[26]. Similarly, oil drilling in Nagaland in the past has led to oil seepage causing damage to villages along oil wells[27]. The argument for ILP as an instrument of protecting locals is thus weak.

---

[26]   Anusua Mukherjee, "Mega Dams in Arunachal Pradesh: A Threat to Its Environment and People," The Hindu, October 20, 2022, https://frontline.thehindu.com/the-nation/mega-dams-in-arunachal-pradesh-a-threat-to-its-environment-and-people/article66004544.ece.

[27] Changpang Oil Spills of Nagaland Feature in Environmental Conflicts and Injustices Map," The Morung Express, January 29, 2016 https://morungexpress.com/changpang-oil-spills-nagaland-feature-environmental-conflicts-and-injustices-map

Limited Effectiveness: The ILP provides some regulatory oversight but does not effectively restrict entry, trade, or residency in practice.

Way Forward

In recent years, there has been a more stringent demand for the implementation of ILP, reflecting the growing need to safeguard local cultures and resources. As state capacity increases, one can anticipate more effective enforcement of ILP rules, ensuring that the system functions as intended. The central government has shown considerable accommodation towards ILP demands and regulations, signaling its support for preserving regional identities. However, ILP should not be weaponized as a cover for xenophobia and racism. Instead, it should be implemented with sensitivity, balancing the need for cultural preservation with inclusivity and national integration, fostering mutual respect and understanding across communities.

MODEL ANSWERS

What is Inner Line Permit?

The Inner Line Permit (ILP) is a special travel document required by Indian citizens to enter certain protected states in India, namely Nagaland, Arunachal Pradesh, Mizoram, and Manipur. This permit is a legal safeguard aimed at preserving the unique cultural identity, land rights, and resources of the indigenous populations in these states.

Explain the importance of ILP to the Nagas.

ILP is crucial in protecting the cultural identity, land rights, and resources from external influences and encroachment. The experience of many tribal societies across the world when they come in contact with more advanced societies results in those tribal societies losing their culture and resources. This has been the case in countries ranging from Canada, USA, and Mexico to Brazil, New Zealand and Australia. Even in India, we have the case of Tripura where tribals have been reduced to a minority in their own land within a few decades. ILP has successfully protected Nagas so far even though there are already complains about how outsiders already dominate businesses in the state.

Do you think ILP is alienating the Nagas from being integrated properly into the Indian union?

India is a continental size country with nearly a billion and a half population. India's strength has been in respecting the diversity of the country. There are often complains about the rest of the country's ignorance of the northeast. This has to be fixed through education. Nagaland can shine within her own corner.

Is ILP fair to Indian citizens who wishes to come to Nagaland?

Sometimes, Indian citizens who wish to visit the northeast complain about the unfairness of ILP in that people from northeast can visit the rest of the country without extra paper works whereas those who wish to travel to states in northeast are burdened with the permit. However, this complain is due to ignorance in understanding the fragility of the northeast which all have relatively small population with low population densities. The risk of these states being overwhelmed by migration is very real, making the ILP a necessary measure to protect the region's cultural identity and demographic balance.

12

Drug Problem in Nagaland

How would you answer?

What are some misconceptions you see regarding drug addiction in Nagaland?

Stigma is often the reason people hide their loved ones using drugs. What measures would you recommend removing the stigma associated with drug use?

As an administrator, what measures can you carry out to eliminate drug use in your jurisdiction?

Are there gaps in the way Nagaland as a state approaches issue of drug use and substance abuse?

Discussion

The temptation of writing a chapter on drug issue in Nagaland is to fill the pages with statistics. However, while data and statistics have their place in a discussion on drug menace in the state, it is equally important not to detach from the everyday experience of a family struggling with addiction. The term "family" here is deliberate in that an individual's struggle with drugs affects the whole family. In Nagaland, the issue of drug use is often linked with spirituality. Thus, when a person falls victim to drug use, the first impulse is to take the "prodigal son" to prayer centres and prayer houses. Drug use is also sometimes labelled a rich man's problem i.e. that only the children of rich parents indulge in drug use. The issue of drug use is also multifaceted; it goes beyond the image of a young man snorting cocaine. We first correct these images before delving into statistics and numbers.

Drug use and family

Drug use destroys families. It sows discord between the couple as also among siblings and parents. Accusations of neglect of spousal care and parental care and accusations of enabling behaviour from spouse and parents run amok. Nagas, often bound by bonds of community with strong emphasis placed on honour and good behaviour, stigma associated with drug use leads to further isolation. No family is rich enough to support drug use and an individual addicted to drugs bring financial ruin to the family. Breakdown of family relations is the first casualty of drug use.

Drug use and spirituality

Often, the first advice to a drug addict to overcome addiction is to find a purpose in life. God is presented as the entity that provides meaning. The care for a drug user in a prayer house is to cast demons out of the person along with times set for prayer. All these could be beneficial in part, but drug use goes beyond spirituality. The element of behavioural formation through compulsion in a rehab, psychiatrists and psychologists to evaluate and guide the patient, counsellors to counsel, doctors to look after the health of the substance user, and the experience and companionship of other drug users to soften the blow of shame are missing in prayer centres. This is not to cast aspersions or condemn prayer centres as inept but to highlight that caring for patients of drug addicts require more specialised people.

The myth of drug use as a rich man's problem

Drug use is also sometimes labelled a rich man's problem. The attitude of the lay people goes "From the money the parents stole, the reward is being reaped through their children's drug use." Nothing can be further from the truth. Drug use does not discriminate against the rich. Perhaps, the problem is more visible among the rich because their children are able to survive longer through proper medical interventions. Regardless, drug use affects all sections of society equally.

Drug use is a sub-set of Substance use

Drug use is often considered a subset of substance use, which encompasses a wide range of substances including alcohol, prescription drugs, and illicit drugs. While drug use typically refers to the non-medical use of illicit drugs, substance use includes any behavior involving substances that may lead to dependence or health issues. Substance abuse goes beyond the image of a young man snorting cocaine.

Broken homes, mental stress, peer pressure, curiosity: Causes of Drug Addiction

A broken home can lead to emotional distress and lack of support leading to drug addiction. Mental stress from personal, academic, or professional pressures also pushes individuals toward drugs as a coping mechanism. Peer pressure, especially among youth, further increases the likelihood of experimenting with substances. Curiosity about the effects of drugs also often leads to initial use, eventually developing into addiction.

Impact of Drugs on Society

Drug addiction reduces productivity as addicts withdraw from work and strains public health with higher treatment costs. It also causes law and order issues, with addicts stealing to fund their habits and suppliers driving crime and violence. As per reports available in public, there are 6,24,000 substance users[28] Nagaland, including 1,11,000 children, with ₹550 crore spent daily on drugs as per 2021 Survey report of the Ministry of Social Justice & Empowerment, Govt of India. Nagaland is also a major route for drugs from Myanmar, with Dimapur as a transit hub.

Ministry of Social Justice and Empowerment's "National Survey on Extent and Pattern of Substance Use in India" (2019)

This comprehensive survey outlines the magnitude and patterns of substance use in India. Key findings include:

a) 16 crore people (14.6%) aged 10-75 years are current alcohol users, with 5.2% dependent.

b) 3.1 crore people use cannabis, and 72 lakh face cannabis-related problem

c) 60 lakh (0.55%) opioid users require treatment

d) 1.18 crore people are non-medical users of sedatives

e) 1.7% of children are inhalant users, with 18 lakh needing help

f) 8.5 lakh people inject drugs (PWID – People Who Inject Drugs).

---

[28] The term substance use encompasses a broader range than just drug addiction, including the misuse of alcohol, prescription medications, and other psychoactive substances.

Statistics from Nagaland

Ministry of Social Justice and Empowerment's Report (2019):
a) Cannabis users: 4.7% from surveyed population
b) Opioid users: 6.5% from surveyed population

Popular Drugs in Nagaland:

1. Sunflower (SF): A cheap and crude form of heroin (opiates), mixed with other drugs like sleeping pills, spasmodart, and alprazolam. It is commonly consumed by sniffing, snorting, or injecting.
2. Spasmoproxyvon (SP): A painkiller containing opioids, which has been commonly abused for its euphoric effects.
3. Relipen (RP): Another pain-relieving drug, also abused for its opioid content.
4. Weed/Marijuana: A psychotropic substance commonly smoked by users before they transition to harder drugs.
5. Brown Sugar: A form of heroin, which is a powerful opioid, leading to intense euphoria followed by tranquillity.

The most popular, however, is SF (sunflower) powder. Its effects include euphoria, followed by severe side effects such as drowsiness, mood swings, and psychotic behaviors. Psychotic behavior refers to a state where a person loses touch with reality, often experiencing delusions (false beliefs) or hallucinations (seeing or hearing things that aren't there). It can also include disorganized thinking, erratic behavior, and difficulty distinguishing between what is real and what is not. In the context of SF (sunflower) powder use, psychotic behavior can manifest as confusion, paranoia, aggression, or irrational thoughts due to the drug's effects on the brain.

The use of Sunflower leads to Health Issues including kidney problems, TB, drug-induced hepatitis, HIV, Hepatitis B and C.

The popularity of Sunflower as a drug stems from its affordability, popular among school children, even as young as 10.

Initiatives and Solutions taken by the Government

Police Crackdown: Dismissal of police officers involved in drug use to ensure accountability and deter misuse within law enforcement.

Operation Good Samaritan: A community-driven campaign in Kiphire aimed at raising awareness and combating drug abuse through collective action.

De-addiction Centers: Opening specialized centers for the rehabilitation of females and young boys affected by drug addiction.

Nasha Mukth Bharat Abhiyan: Anti-drug campaigns across various districts in Nagaland focusing on prevention, demand reduction, and public awareness.

Increase in De-addiction Centers: Ministry of Social Justice & Empowerment plans to increase the number of de-addiction centers to improve access to treatment and recovery services.

Recommendations:

1. Spread awareness about drug dangers, especially among youths.
2. Implement drug prevention programs in schools.
3. Provide medication-assisted treatment and counselling.
4. Initiate community outreach programs to combat drug menace.

What are some misconceptions you see regarding drug addiction in Nagaland?

There are several misconceptions regarding drug use in Nagaland. One of the first misconception is to see drug use as a spiritual and a moral problem rather than as a behavioural or psychological problem. A person with drug problem is thus taken to prayer centres first before taking them to hospitals, counsellors, psychiatrists and rehabs. Church and prayer centres have their place but unless there are qualified counsellors, the church is not equipped to deal with them. Also, the church is too crowded to provide focused attention which the addict needs.

The second misconception is to label drug-use a rich man's problem not realising it affects all sections of society equally.

Stigma is often the reason people hide their loved ones using drugs. What measures would you recommend removing the stigma associated drug use?

Organising awareness programs in collaboration with civil societies in educational institutions and churches would go a long way to reducing stigma. In such programs, drug problems should be highlighted not as a moral failing but as a health and psychological issue.

As an administrator, what measures can you carry out to eliminate drug use in your jurisdiction?

As an administrator, several measures can be taken to eliminate drug use in one's jurisdiction. This include raising awareness programs on prevention and care, strictly enforcing laws to prevent drug trafficking and distribution, encouraging treatment and providing provisions for rehabilitation through removal of stigma against rehabs and through community engagement.

Are there gaps in the way Nagaland as a state approaches issue of drug use and substance abuse?

Yes, there are several gaps. There are limited prevention programs, inadequate treatment facilities, insufficient law enforcement, lack of community support, and the stigmatisation associated with drug use and treatment is still high.

13

"We, the people": Examining Ramifications of Competing Claims to Naga Representation

Competing Claims to Naga Representation:

1. Naga tribal apex bodies
2. Naga political groups
3. The Government of Nagaland

How would you answer?

What do you think is the fundamental problem that Nagaland's economy faces?

Would you agree that ceasefire has led to more problems?

What is peace dividend?

What problems will Nagaland face once the Naga political issue is resolved in terms of its institutions? Will it become a paradise on earth?

How does the existence of multiple political groups go against the definition of the state given by Max Weber?

Discussion

The phrase "We, the People" originates from the preamble of the United States Constitution, symbolizing the idea that government derives its authority from the consent of the governed. It represents a commitment to democracy and the collective sovereignty of the citizens in establishing and upholding the nation's framework of laws and governance. It underscores unity and shared purpose among the people in creating a just and equitable society.

In populist governments, the phrase "We, the People" is often used to emphasize a direct connection between the ruling leadership and the masses, bypassing traditional institutions like legislatures or judiciary systems. Populist leaders frame themselves as the voice of the "true people" against perceived elites or outsiders. This can lead to the concentration of power in the executive and an erosion of institutional checks and balances, as populism focuses more on majoritarian sentiment and less on the pluralistic and inclusive nature of constitutional democracies.

Competing Claims to Naga Representation

A combination of different factors give rise to three claimants asserting to represent the Nagas with powerful rationales behind those claims. These are:

1. Naga tribal apex bodies
2. Naga political groups
3. The Government of Nagaland

The tribal apex bodies represent the socio-cultural aspiration of the people. The Naga political groups have a historical claim to politically represent the Nagas. Theoretically, as a constitutional democracy, the Government of Nagaland represents "We, the people" since the government is elected by the people. What effects these conflicting claims have on Naga society will emerge clearly as each claim is examined closely.

Tribal Apex Bodies as Representation of "We, the People"

Tribal apex bodies, deeply rooted in Naga society, can be seen as traditional embodiments of the phrase "We, the People" within the unique socio-cultural context of the region. These bodies represent the collective identity and voice of each tribe, ensuring that the interests and welfare of their members are safeguarded. Unlike modern democratic governments, their legitimacy stems not from elections but from shared customs, collective consent, and respect for traditional authority.

As representatives of their tribes, these apex bodies mediate disputes, protect members from external threats (such as political or economic exploitation), and preserve cultural practices and values. Their influence reflects a form of participatory governance that predates the introduction of modern constitutional democracy. In this sense, they act as custodians of a collective identity that resonates with the spirit of *We, the People* by emphasizing communal solidarity, shared responsibility, and the protection of tribal sovereignty.

However, this traditional representation is not without challenges. While these bodies uphold values such as honesty and communal bonds, their adherence to certain customs has led to conflicts with progressive ideas, such as gender equality. In this tension, tribal apex bodies highlight the complexities of aligning customary governance with modern democratic ideals.

We, the people of Nagaland, ENPO, CNTC, NTC

Leadership tussles and suspicions along tribal lines was a big issue in the Naga fight for self-determination. The othering of other tribes has however occurred mostly as a result of conflict over government resources. The formation of Nagaland Tribes Council (NTC) was with the objective of fighting for the interest of Naga tribes residing in Nagaland. The accusation about the Naga Hoho and other apex bodies is that its vision of a pan-Naga political entity, Nagalim, comes at the expense of Nagas from Nagaland. Such a view, however, is expressed cautiously, as it is widely condemned as narrow-minded. The ENPO and ENSF have become formidable organisations in Nagaland in the last few decades. The ENPO's demand for a Frontier Nagaland Territory rests on the argument that Nagaland's economic development has seen regional imbalance with the ENPO-inhabited areas trailing far behind the rest of the state. This inequality according to them, arises from unequal access to government resources. The CNTC, argues that tribes like the Chakhesangs are no longer in need of quota reservations in government services.

Naga Political Groups

Naga political groups form the second pillar asserting ownership of "We, the People." Their claim is deeply rooted in the historic role they played in the Naga struggle for self-determination. The formation and growth of pan-Naga consciousness and the idea of a Naga nation were significantly shaped by the Naga National Council (NNC) under various leaders. The Plebiscite of 1951, which demonstrated the collective will of the Naga people to remain free and sovereign, was a landmark event organized by the NNC.

The Naga political movement extends beyond Nagaland, encompassing pan-Naga representation in other Naga-inhabited areas. Over the decades, it has played a crucial role in defending the rights of the Naga people. However, divisions have emerged within the movement, with multiple groups claiming to represent the Naga cause. While the events that led to these splits are not examined here, the impacts of these divisions are significant. As of September 2024, there are reportedly 26 Naga political groups in the state, reflecting both the legacy of the movement and the fragmentation within its ranks.

Economic impact of multiple political groups

This multiplication of groups has complicated the Naga peace process, with multiple factions holding differing views on autonomy, sovereignty, and negotiations with the Indian government. The presence of many groups has also led to challenges in maintaining unity among the Naga people and has contributed to internal conflicts. Monetary demands in the form of "taxes" or "donations" made to businesses, contractors and even to the government has undermined economic stability.

The effects of such practices are broad and impactful:

Increase in Cost of Doing Business: Extortion drives up the cost of doing business, as business have to allocate additional resources for protection or pay illegal demands. This added financial burden deter new businesses from entering the market and strain existing ones.

Decrease in Profit Margins: With increased costs due to extortion, businesses experience reduced profit margins. Higher operational costs often lead to lower profitability, affecting the sustainability and growth potential of local enterprises.

Uncertainty and Fear: The practice of extortion creates an environment of uncertainty and fear. Business owners and investors are wary of potential threats and unpredictable demands, which undermine their confidence and willingness to invest or expand.

Increase in Cost of Products and Decreased Demand: The higher costs incurred due to extortion are often passed on to consumers, leading to increased prices for products. As a result, demand decrease, affecting sales and further impacting the local economy.

Negative Impact on External Investment: Extortion sends a negative message to outside investors. Perceptions of instability and corruption deter potential investors from considering Nagaland as a viable location for investment, hindering economic development and job creation.

Breeding Corruption: Extortion for funds contribute to a culture of corruption. Funds intended for development are embezzled by local officials who then blame Naga political groups.

Increased Central Government Funding: Rightly or wrongly, the common populace believes that in response to the challenges posed by extortion and its economic impacts, there is increased funding from the central government to support local development. A fear one hears (misguided or not) is that the central government might reduce resource allocation for the state once the Naga political issue is solved.

Ceasefire, Peace Dividend and Gun Culture

The ceasefire between the Indian military and the Naga political groups as well as the cessation of hostilities between the different factions of the Naga political groups have brought much respite to the people. The human rights violation and the excessive use of force by the Indian military, and Naga factions killing each other in scores took place not a long time ago. When Indian leaders visit Nagaland, the appeal to the warring factions often was that Nagas could reap peace dividend once the Naga political issue was solved. The idea was that the uncertain political environment and the atmosphere of hatred and killings was curtailing the economic potential of the state.

After nearly three decades since the 1997 cease-fire between the NSCN-IM and the Government of India, it is fair to say that peace has not brought about the economic windfall as predicted. Thirty years is also long enough to produce a young generation whose memory of violence have faded. The ceasefire however has produced an incentive structure where it is all gains and no pains to join the different political groups. Fear of life and limb was real enough to dissuade young people from joining underground groups. Cessation of hostilities on all counts have removed this fear. With easily procured guns, and increasing number of groups, extortion demands have increased.

Government of Nagaland

The Government of Nagaland is formed by the elected members of legislative assembly. At the state level, it represents "We, the People" as given in the preamble to the Indian constitution. The Government of Nagaland has control over the social, political, economic and civil life of residents of Nagaland. Since Nagaland was formed as a result of a political agreement between the Indian union and the people of Nagaland, the Nagaland Legislative Assembly of which the Government of Nagaland has control of, enjoys special powers. The responsibility for maintaining law and order and bring about economic development rests with the Government of Nagaland. The allegiance of the members of the legislative assembly however is shaped by Naga history, its people and the Indian constitution. While members swear allegiance to the Indian constitution, they do not want to be caught on the wrong side of history. Members thus openly say that they would be open to vacating their seats for an alternative arrangement between the Naga political groups and the Indian government. The government sees itself as the facilitator. "We, the people" are burdened with collection and extortion. The Government of Nagaland that constitutionally represents "We, the People" do not have the conviction to carry out the mandate of law and order given to it every 5 years labelling issues of extortion as a political problem. The leadership in the Government of Nagaland faces a conflict of conviction – aspirations of people fighting for Naga self-determination and following the Indian constitution.

Bastard State Called Nagaland

A bastard child used to mean a child born out of wedlock. A child born to unmarried parents was considered illegitimate for a long time. The same term in Chokri Chakhesang dialect is '*Tekhrünu*.' *Tekhrünu* also means a she-dog that has given birth outside of its mating season. Socially progressive sensibilities in recent years have avoided such language.

The Naga demand for self-determination enjoyed wide public support. When statehood was granted, the state was perceived by many as temporary and even illegitimate. The state was a *tekhrünu* in the eyes of the public. To many, statehood was the ploy of the central government to divide and rule. The hand of Indian intelligence in winning over certain Naga leaders was at times given serious consideration. This fuelled suspicions that the central government's granting of statehood had been a strategic move to undermine the Naga independence movement by creating internal divisions. As a result, the legitimacy of the state was questioned by many Nagas who saw it as a compromise that failed to address their core demand for full sovereignty. In everyday language, Nagas received only 50 paise when they were demanding one full rupee.

Even after 60 years of statehood, the state has not fully honoured people who gave their lives for statehood. Even politicians do not renounce the popular demand for sovereignty.

Statehood was also a stick with which the Indian government could use against the popular demand for sovereignty. Morarji Desai asserted to Phizo in London in their 1977 meeting that the Nagas had come demanding statehood, and the Indian government had granted it to them.

A result of all these is that people do not identify with their government. Unlike the fervent support in social media seen for the central government in India or in the U.S., this kind of affinity is rarely observed in Nagaland.

Extortion as a challenge to state's authority

Max Weber defined the state as "a human community that (successfully) claims the monopoly of the legitimate use of physical force within a given territory." Monopoly of violence means that the government has the sole right to use coercive force to impose order including imprisonment, legal punishment and physical violence. Legitimate means it should be sanctioned by law, and recognised by the people as lawful.

Coercive power of the state include the ability to collect taxation. A tax is a compulsory financial charge or levy imposed by a government on individuals or entities (such as businesses) to fund public expenditures, services, and government activities. It is the sole remit of the state represented by the government. Other actors, organisations and businesses can collect fees, rent, royalties, and other forms of payments, but these are not considered taxes. Taxes are specifically mandated and enforced by the state, reflecting its authority to regulate and collect revenue to support its functions and obligations. According to Article 265 of Indian Constitution "No tax shall be levied or collected except by authority of law". Any collection compelled by any authority is a violation of this article, including any forced collection by the national political groups in the state. In as much as the mandated government is unable to stop such collection, it is an effective challenge on the authority of the government.

Where does the buck stop in Nagaland?

Harry S Truman, the 33rd president of the United States, had a written note on his table that read "The Buck Stops Here." It was to remind himself and others that he was in charge of the country, that he was responsible and accountable for any actions undertaken by his administration. It acted as a reminder that where there were lapses in the country, he was the one responsible to fix it.

On different issues in the state, the Government of Nagaland often expresses helplessness, leading one to wonder who is in charge of the state. On law and order, the government expresses helplessness because of Naga political issue. On women reservation and women's rights, the government expresses helplessness on account of opposition by tribal hohos. On pollution and environmental standards, it blames lack of civic sense by the common people. On poor infrastructure, it blames Nagaland's topography and land ownership system. On lifting alcohol prohibition, it blames opposition by the NBCC. On its state of finance, it blames the non-revenue generation from the state. No government in India or outside expresses as much helplessness as is done by the Government of Nagaland.

Way Forward: State Capacity Building

For effective governance, the Government of Nagaland needs to strengthen its capacity. This can be achieved through proper recruitment practices, as past instances of flawed hiring have contributed significantly to the state's current challenges.

Strengthening governance begins with the fair and consistent implementation of existing protocols, rules, and regulations. Furthermore, effective and reliable service delivery is essential for building public trust and fostering a more cooperative relationship between the government and its citizens. There are many areas where additional resource spending is required, however, the perception that the government is inefficient and corrupt has to go before people start contributing. Resource management is thus another critical area.

The fundamental difficulty of governance in Nagaland, apart from the challenges posed by the other two pillars – civil society and Naga political groups – is that Nagas are well-educated and increasingly aware of their rights while the state lacks the capacity to ensure the fulfillment of those rights.

Model Answers

What do you think is the fundamental problem that Nagaland's economy faces?

There are many problems that Nagaland's economy faces, such as unemployment, land ownership issues, the Naga political problem, over-dependence on the central government, and lack of investment. However, the biggest issue is low state capacity. The government does not have the vision, will, or strength to bring about meaningful reforms and development initiatives that could address these challenges effectively and sustainably. This lack of capacity stifles progress and prevents the state from harnessing its full economic potential.

Would you agree that ceasefire has led to more problems?

The argument against ceasefires is that it has led to more extortions. Since entry to the political groups have not been banned, with no fear of losing one's life, recruits have been easily found. With freely available guns, there is no proportionate disincentive against extortion. However, the argument for ceasefire is that the losing of lives which was rampant just 15 years ago has fallen to a great extent, thanks to the efforts made by the Forum for Naga Reconciliation (FNR). The climate of fear, the fear that fightings can occur anytime has fallen to a great extent. For the young generation, in fact, the shadow of gun violence has rapidly disappeared. The goal should be to implement ceasefire rules more effectively, and to discourage new recruits.

What is peace dividend?

The "peace dividend" in Nagaland refers to the economic and social benefits expected from resolving the region's conflicts, including increased investment, improved governance, and social harmony. With peace, resources can be redirected from security to development, fostering long-term stability and growth.

What problems will Nagaland face once the Naga political issue is resolved in terms of its institutions? Will it become a paradise on earth?

While the underground groups pose a serious problem to the development of the state, they are only one part of the problem among several. The governmental authority seen as a legal rational authority is still very weak. It has not ingrained itself enough into the collective psyche of the people. People view the government as an alien institution. Combined a toothless government with the well-organised communities in different forms such as clan, village, and tribe, and identity groups taking the guise of civil societies, the state as an entity cannot assert its power. While the rule of law demands that the government does not abuse its power, and that there be checks and balances, the state/government itself needs to have power before we discuss taming and limiting its power. In Nagaland, even a well-organised village can bring the state to its knees.

No, Nagaland will not become a paradise on earth.

Follow up Question

Why is it important for the state to possess power?

It is important for the state to posses power simply for things to be done. During COVID-19 Pandemic, when countries were being assessed on how well they were responding to the crisis, questions began to be raised on which type of governments were doing better to respond to the crisis – democratic or authoritarian. The broad conclusion was that it was not so much about whether the country was democratic or authoritarian but whether the state capacity was strong. Broadly, the most basic function of a state is to maintain law and order, protect its borders, and enable citizens to go about their day-to-day activities. State functions have expanded to provide what are called public goods[29] and merit goods[30]. All these require a combination of hard power as well as economic power. In many western societies, states are able to achieve them through a

---

[29] Public goods are goods which are non-excludable (cannot prevent people from using them) and non-rivalrous (one person's use does not diminish availability for others), such as national defense, public parks, and clean air.

[30] Merit goods are goods or services that are deemed socially desirable by the government or society, often under-consumed if left to market forces, such as education, healthcare, and public libraries, typically provided or subsidized to ensure equitable access.

combination of historical process as well as through active state building.

How does the existence of multiple political groups go against the definition of the state given by Max Weber?

Max Weber defined the state as "a human community that (successfully) claims the monopoly of the legitimate use of physical force within a given territory." The existence of multiple actors able to assert its power goes against the definition of the state as given by Max Weber. In Nagaland, the government is only one of the actors imposing its rule on the people. Even if the government recognises that its authority is being challenged, instead of asserting its power, it will seek to negotiate. In a democracy, there is room for negotiation but not when its authority is fundamentally undermined.

14

Free Movement Regime (FMR)

Explain the details of free movement regime?

Are you in favour of Free Movement Regime?

As an administrator, if the central government compels you to shut the border, what will you do if the local populace is in favour of keeping the border open?

Do you think the arguments of the central government to restrict movement of people in border areas are valid?

Why is the Free Movement Regime said to have begun in 2018 even though tribals have been free to move across the border as early as the 1950s?

What is the official position of the state government on free movement regime?

Discussion

In 1948, the then Burmese Government allowed tribes from neighbouring countries to enter Burma without passports, provided they lived within 25 miles or 40 km of the border. The tribes were also allowed to carry a head-load of goods. Additionally, Myanmar citizens were permitted to stay in India for 72 hours, while Indians could stay in Myanmar for 24 hours. This arrangement became known as the Free Movement Regime (FMR). India followed suit. Thus, on September 26, 1950, the Ministry of Home Affairs issued a notification amending the Passport (Entry into India) Rules, exempting hill tribes within 40 km (25 miles) of the India-Myanmar border from needing a passport or visa to enter India.

However, the FMR was used by different political groups in India from Naga, Mizo, and Meitei communities fighting against the Government of India who used the border to cross into Myanmar, receive arms training, and return to India to carry out attacks. The poorly guarded border and FMR provisions made it easy for them to do so, threatening regional security.

In response, the Indian government decided to tighten the FMR. In August 1968, the Ministry of Home Affairs introduced a permit system for crossing the Myanmar border, requiring both Indian and Burmese citizens to carry permits. This system remained in place for the next 40 years.

During the 1990s and early 2000s, the security situation in the Northeast worsened, with increasing incidents of drug trafficking, arms smuggling, and the political groups moving across the India-Myanmar border. To address this, in 2004, India reduced the FMR limits to 16 km and restricted border crossings to three designated points: Pangsau in Arunachal Pradesh, Moreh in Manipur, and Zokhawthar in Mizoram.

Due to continued misuse of the Free Movement Regime (FMR), India proposed a formal agreement with Myanmar in 2014. After negotiations, the Agreement on Land Border Crossing was signed on 11 May 2018. Under this agreement, residents within 16 km of the border in both countries are issued border passes, which they must carry at all times when crossing the border. They are allowed to stay on the other side for up to 14 days.

In January 2024, during ongoing ethnic violence in Manipur, the Government of India announced plans to end the Free Movement Regime (FMR) due to concerns about illegal immigration, drug trafficking, and arms smuggling. The Government of Mizoram and civil society groups in Manipur and Nagaland opposed the move. Despite the opposition, the Indian government suspended the FMR on February 8, 2024, while it negotiates with Myanmar about permanently ending the agreement.

The issue of fencing the border took more serious turns during the ethnic tensions in Manipur in 2023 between Kukis and Meiteis. The accusation of the Meiteis is that there has been an influx of Kuki migrants from Myanmar into Manipur leading to drastic population increase of Kukis in Manipur. The Meiteis use census data to support their point. As per the news site from Manipur epao.net, according to the 1881 census, the old Kuki population was 8,180 which increased to 63,332 according to 2011 census showing an increased of 774% or 7.74 times. The nomadic section of Kuki-Zo-Chin population however increased from 17,204 in 1881 to 4,48,214 in 2011, an increase of 2605% or 26 times[31].

Arguments for FMR

1. **Cultural Ties:** The FMR facilitates deep cultural and social ties among communities on both sides of the border, including shared languages, traditions, and family connections. These ties have historically facilitated cross-border interactions. The

---

[31] K. Yugindro Singh, M. Manihar Singh & Sh. Janaki Sharma, "Abnormal population growth of Chin-Kuki-Zo in Manipur since 1881", *epao.net*, February 12, 2024, https://e-pao.net/epSubPageExtractor.asp?src=manipur.Census_of_Manipur.Abnormal_population_growth_of_Chin_Kuki_Zo_in_Manipur_since_1881

Naga people live across the India-Myanmar border, and the FMR impacts their ability to maintain connections and travel between their communities on either side of the border.

2. **Colonial Hangover:** The colonial legacy of arbitrarily drawn borders continues to affect border policies and relations, with the FMR being a remnant of colonial-era agreements that did not fully account for ethnic and cultural realities.

3. Borders as Not Lines but Territories

The Home Ministry's decision to fence the border and discontinue Free Movement Regime is a move against conventional wisdom gained in recent years. It is also a shift from calls made by its own intelligentsia.

Views on international boundaries have evolved over the years. In international relations, the concept of territory is increasingly reimagined beyond traditional state-centric views. Territory is now seen as a product of social relations rather than just fixed geographical space. The calls to reimagine its borders have echoes at the top echelon of power in India. According to Shyam Saran, former Foreign Secretary of India:

> "The conventional view of national territorial boundaries is that these are, or ought to be, strong and durable fences, safeguarding the country from hostile external forces. Passage across these fences must, therefore, be through tightly controlled, carefully regulated and narrow gateways. This is an outdated notion in the modern world and the time has come for us to begin to look at our borders as "connectors" or "transmission belts", which bring us closer to

our neighbours in a mutually beneficial embrace rather than as impenetrable walls behind which we insulate ourselves.[32]"

Government's logic against FMR

The Central Government argue that the FMR must be regulated to address security and economic concerns.

Drug Problem

The Northeast proximity to the Golden Triangle and the use of the northeast as a transit to drug transport is a real concern when it comes to continuing FMR. The problem is made worse due to collusion between politicians, political groups and drug mafia using unfenced border for easy transport of drug. The involvement of local youth in both drug consumption and illegal substance transport makes the problem more dire. Drug use among youth is a serious dent on the human resource of the border communities. Questions, however, need to be asked:

1.   Is FMR solely to blame?

2.   Will removing FMR solve the problem of drug use and usage of northeast as drug transit points?

On both questions, it is easy to blame FMR. However, the experience of other countries have shown that fencing the border is not always the solution. The issue of tackling drug menace requires a nuanced approach of breaking up the nexus of political groups, politicians and drug mafia through smart policing, upgrading border infrastructure through the use of technology, providing jobs to local youth and strengthening the institutions governing border areas. The villages along the borders should be strengthened to tackle drug menace

---

[32] Shyam Saran, "Re-imagining India's borders", *Business Standard, January 20, 2013, https://www.business-standard.com/article/opinion/shyam-saran-re-imagining-india-s-borders-111062400025_1.html*

through community engagement, fast-tracked courts, infrastructure development and financial incentives.

Illegal Migration

India has grown much faster economically than Myanmar in the last few decades. The institutions in India are also more developed. Myanmar has been a basket case, riddled with problems from its extractive institutions, mostly the Myanmarese military. The Myanmarese government inability to assert power, bring stability and deliver economic growth has been well-known. People from India who have crossed over into the Myanmarese territory have often highlighted the stark contrast between the Indian villages and Myanmarese inhabitants. FMR by enabling free movement of people can thus easily lead to mass migration. One issue with mass migration in a democracy is the use of illegal migrants as a vote bank, with politicians focusing on short terms gains over long term stability.

Insurgency Problems

In the past, China has been known to support political groups in the northeast fighting for independence or secession through trainings, arm and intelligence logistics, financial supports and ideological brainwashing. The Chinese follow a policy of "bleed India through million cuts[33]." The Myanmarese route is the most common route used by different political groups to reach China. The FMR is sometimes blamed for this.

---

[33] Rinku Khumukcham, "RN Ravi's Take on China's Factor in India's North Eastern Insurgency," Imphal Times, July 31, 2020, https://www.imphaltimes.com/guest-column/rn-ravi-s-take-on-china-s-factor-in-india-s-north-eastern-insurgency/.

Way Forward

The FMR is a complicated issue. A balanced nuanced approach should be pursued in policy-making for the border regions.

MODEL ANSWERS

Explain the details of free movement regime?

The FMR is a mutually agreed arrangement between India and Myanmar that allows tribes living along the border on either side to travel up to 16 km inside the other country without a visa.

Are you in favour of Free Movement Regime?

Yes. The lines dividing the two countries were arbitrarily drawn dividing even homes and tight-knit communities. To do away with the FMR would be unfair and uncalled for.

As an administrator, if the central government compels you to shut the border, what will you do if the local populace is in favour of keeping the border open?

As an administrator, my primary duty is to uphold the directives of the central government, as it holds the authority in matters of national policy and security. While I may understand and empathize with the local populace's preference for keeping the border open, it is my responsibility to implement the government's decisions, ensuring that any action taken aligns with national interests and security protocols. However, I would engage in open communication with the community to explain the reasons behind the decision and seek to mitigate any negative impact through supportive measures.

Do you think the arguments of the central government to restrict movement of people in border areas are valid?

In public domain, there is no record of the central government conducting proper study and consultation on FMR. Proper studies, consultations with the local populace, and ways to solve problems should be explored before alienating the people. India wants to spread its sphere of influence as an emerging power and cannot do so by cocooning itself further.

Why is the Free Movement Regime said to have begun in 2018 even though tribals have been free to move across the border as early as the 1950s?

The FMR was formalised only in 2018 as part of an agreement with the Myanmarese government.

What is the official position of the state government on free movement regime?

The Nagaland Government is opposed to scrapping the FMR and fencing the Indo-Myanmar border. The Nagaland Government's official position is that the central government should work out regulations for movement of people across the boundary in consultation with the people inhabiting the border areas, and for suitably bringing in the village council authorities concerned in the entire system of regulation

15

Proliferation of Civil Societies and Identity groups

How would you answer?

Why do civil societies in Nagaland continue to proliferate despite widespread complains about the excessive number of such groups? Is hunger for power a good explanation?

Is there any positive contribution of civil society groups in Nagaland?

Do we need more civil societies in Nagaland? Justify your answer.

Discussion

Nagas have a thousand and one civil societies. The proliferation of civil societies have led to complains from several quarters:

1. **Excessive monetary collections and fund-raising activities without commensurate returns to members.** The

complains of many is that funds are raised without traces of those resources being spent on productive activities.

2. **Sacrifice of time and talents in unproductive areas**. Instead of working in offices or spending leisure time enjoying one's hobby or spending quality time with one's family and friends, a person's time and energy is spent attending meetings, bringing out resolutions, chalking out programs etc.

Civil societies in more matured democracies are often formed for raising specific issues or causes or for opposing certain actions of the government. They are formed for raising the cause of education, health, environment, economic development, art and culture, gender equality, among others, and removal of issues such as poverty and other social evils. Such civil societies are not active in Nagaland.

Why has civil societies proliferated in Nagaland?

Almost everyone is of the opinion that there is an excess of civil societies in Nagaland. However, civil societies have only multiplied. Why is this the case? In a survey by the Morung Express, proliferation of civil societies in Nagaland was mostly attributed to greed for power and wealth[34]. Though this may be the case in certain prominent civil societies, this is not true of the majority of civil societies. Civil societies in Nagaland are mostly identity-based. In many cases, leaders in many civil societies participate reluctantly.

---

[34] What Kind of Effect Is the Increasing Number of Naga Civil Society Organisations Having on the Nagas? Give Reasons," Weekly Poll Result, April 6, 2024, https://morungexpress.com/what-kind-of-effect-is-the-increasing-number-of-naga-civil-society-organisations-having-on-the-nagas-give-reasons

Funds are also not abundant. Greed for power and wealth are thus not good explanation.

When societies go through quick transitions, lopsided development of certain institutions take place. An example cited often is the case of African countries where the formation of many independent countries and the easy supply of guns and ammunitions led to the lopsided development of the military, and consequently to the formation of dictatorships. In the case of Nagaland, this lopsided development has taken the form of identity-consciousness and the formation of identity groups.

Naga society's transition from simple village-based societies to identification as tribes, the formation of statehood and development of urban centres have led to proliferation of identity-based civil society groups. Increase in income, education and development of means of communication have facilitated this proliferation. Formation and strengthening of identity groups take place when the groups can organise themselves. Thus, even in Nagaland, the first identity groups were from the more educated and richer tribes like the Ao Student' Union, and the Angami Students' Union.

A Naga individual is usually a member of the following groups depending on his stage in life:

1. Village's group
2. Village students' union (or a village's welfare group if he is a high-class government employee)
3. Village youth's group (or women's group depending on the age bracket)
4. Clan's group
5. Residents of an urban center like Kohima or Dimapur will be additionally in the following groups

        a. village's group of that town
        b. village students' group of that town
        c. Students' group of the tribe
        d. Students' group of the tribe of the college
6. Tribe's group
7. Tribe youth's group
8. Gazetted or government employees' group
9. Scholars' group or literature board of some sort
10. Local church
11. Local church children's/youth's/women's/father's group
12. Church's group at the level of the tribe
13. Church's group at the state level

These different groups depending on their capacity will raise funds to construct building, go for picnics, have freshers' days, celebrate occasions such as silver jubilee, and golden jubilee. Since an individual by default becomes a member of the identity group, he finds it difficult to escape any of it. The contribution the individual makes for each group could be minimal but there are enough groups, and the contributions made are frequent enough to significantly pinch the pockets of the contributors.

Consequences of proliferation of civil societies:

In the same Morung Express opinion poll, divisions among Nagas have been mentioned as a consequence of the proliferation of civil societies. Though this has not been elaborated in the poll, the explanation can be provided thus: A civil society leader has to prove utility to its members. At the slightest provocation, the group pick up fights. Endless condemnations for unlawful actions and a plethora of congratulatory messages on print and digital media has marked the Naga society in recent years.

Do we need more civil societies?

The sad answer to this question is an emphatic "Yes". We need more civil societies, just not the kind we already have. Take the case of Civil Engineering Association of Nagaland (CEAN). Through minimal actions, it has been able to highlight and rectify many wrongs in the way the Nagaland Public Services Commission conducts its recruitment exams. We need many similar action-oriented civil societies rather than identity-based civil societies.

Is there any benefit of the many civil societies we have?

There are broadly three pillars of power in the state: Naga political groups, state government and civil society groups. Civil societies serve as a bulwark against the tyranny of the political groups and as a bargaining unit for its constituents in their dealings with the state government. The political groups once enjoyed legitimacy and popular support. However, at present, guns owned by the political groups have been used to extort money; the multiplication of political groups have made the extortions unbearable. Naga civil societies such as tribal hohos and tribe students' groups enjoy popular support. They represent, in many cases, the voice of the people. They ensure that political groups do not harass its members. Constitutionally, the state government is the mandated authority. However, because Naga experience with modern state institutions were very recent, a full embrace of government institutions is yet to take place. Government institutions are still foreign. However, the government commands the largest share of resources in the state. As such, ensuring equitable distribution and compelling the government to play by the rules are important functions of civil societies in the state.

Since civil societies enjoy popular support, they have also been able to mediate successfully in cases of conflicts. Where misunderstandings or unlawful activities take place between two communities, civil societies are often the first responder in establishing peace.

Civil societies also play important roles in recognising the achievements of its members. When a non-Naga friend of the author got a scientist position abroad, there was no congratulatory message of any kind from any civil society organisation. Such a scenario would be unthinkable in Nagaland. Are the images of our handsome and pretty faces put forth by civil society organisations when we achieve something worth all the trouble we go through to maintain them?

MODEL ANSWERS

Why do civil societies in Nagaland continue to proliferate despite widespread complaints about the excessive number of such groups? Is hunger for power a good explanation?

Naga society is a society in fast-paced transition. Our mindset is still tribal though a modern government has been introduced to us supported by generous endowment from the central government. Our ability to organise ourselves have improved tremendously through increased income and modern means of communication. A combination of our tribalistic mindset and improved ability to organise ourselves have led to excessive proliferation of civil societies in Nagaland.

Hunger for power is not a good explanation as many people participate unwillingly.

Is there any positive contribution of civil society groups in Nagaland?

In more matured democracies, civil societies serve as a bulwark against the tyranny of the state. In Nagaland, civil societies serve as bulwark against the tyranny of different political groups. In a state like Nagaland where trends for institutional practices are still being set, civil societies exist to protect the interests of its group members.

Do we need more civil societies in Nagaland? Justify your answer.

Yes, Nagaland needs more civil societies meant for promotion of social goods such as education, health, and environment while fighting against social ills like corruption, poverty and pollution.

16

Agricultural Challenges and Opportunities in Nagaland

How would you answer?

The Chief Minister in his 78th Independence Day speech, 2024 said nearly 71% of Nagas are practicing agriculture in one form or another. How is it then that Nagaland is not self-sufficient in anything? Is it a problem?

What do you think is the biggest problem facing agriculture in Nagaland?

What is the importance of agriculture sector in an economy?

What is organic agriculture? Is it feasible in Nagaland?

What is the impact of climate change on agriculture in Nagaland?

Should we encourage National Mission on Oil Seeds and Oil Palm in Nagaland?

Discussion

The importance of agriculture in an economy are several: they provide food and nutritional security for the populace, provide raw materials to several industries and provide employment to the people. The challenges to agriculture in Nagaland include low productivity, lack of access to finance, and inability to produce for the market. The tragedy of agriculture in Nagaland is that inspite of the significant workforce engaged in it, the contribution of agriculture to state's GSDP is miniscule. At the same time, it is unable to achieve sufficiency in majority of the food products. The government has a dedicated agriculture ministry with the department of agriculture being one of the most important departments formulating policies and channelling funds from the central government and implementing different schemes. However, the general apathy associated with governance in the state leaves one of its biggest mark in agriculture. Nagas had a lot of pride in being associated with agriculture and even now it is the default past time of the rich to set up horticulture projects as investment and hobby. As per data available for 2011-12, 61% of Nagaland's workforce is engaged in agriculture.

For the state to develop, it cannot ignore the agriculture sector as majority of the people are involved in it. It has several competitive advantages:

High Land-Person Ratio: Nagaland has a high ratio of land per capita, with most land being owned by families, eliminating the costs associated with land leasing and rent. Nagaland's mix of plain and hill topography is a potential for growing a variety of agricultural crops.

Potential for Commercial Agriculture[35]: Nagaland's varied agro-climatic conditions support a range of crops, including fruits, vegetables, spices, mushrooms, and tuber crops, as well as exotic varieties like dragon fruit, broccoli, kale, zucchini, and asparagus, making it ideal for export. Horticulture offers eco-friendly farming options with products like squash, juices, and pickles, while

---

[35] Rupa Dutta and Hemendra Chauhan, "Ploughing Ahead: Exploring Nagaland's Agriculture Potential," Nagaland Post (Dimapur), April 6, 2023

apiculture, with a honey production potential of 10,000 MT annually, taps into the growing demand for natural sweeteners. Sericulture benefits from traditional silk farming, with government schemes promoting silk reeling and weaving. Livestock farming, dairy, fisheries, and aquaculture thrive due to abundant water resources, while bamboo, with applications in tools, construction, and energy, and coconut plantations covering 15,000 hectares, add economic value. The state's largely organic practices further position it as a hub for high-value and export-oriented agriculture.

Infrastructure and Institutional Needs

1. **Storage Facilities:** Adequate storage facilities are essential for a successful agricultural sector. The non-utilisation of existing storage facilities however has been an issue.
2. **Transportation Infrastructure:** Efficient transportation systems are needed to move large quantities of produce.
3. **Market Mechanisms:** Mechanisms to procure produce at fair prices and find markets, ensuring farmers' products are sold at proper prices are being sorely missed.
4. **Crop Insurance and Minimum Procurement Prices:** These measures are crucial to support farmers and ensure their financial security.

MODEL ANSWERS

The Chief Minister in his 78th independence day speech, 2024 said 71% of Nagas practice agriculture in one form or another. How is it then that Nagaland is not self-sufficient in anything? Is it a problem?

The problem is not lack of self-sufficiency in certain food products, it is the lack of self-sufficiency in every food product. The nature of our topography and climate of our state means we lack comparative advantage in certain food products such as rice. However, that we are unable to produce any marketable surplus in any crop leads to a scenario where 71% of our population is still dependent directly or indirectly on agriculture, and at the same time, we have to import all food products. The nature of agriculture market is very complicated. Countries do not want to depend on others for their food needs. Since we cannot shift our workforce dramatically away from agriculture overnight, if we want to improve our farm productivity, we have to up-skill ourselves to become a part of the agriculture value chain. However, that will require significant structural upgradation which the state is incapable of at the moment. The state of agriculture for the vast majority of practitioners is not very bright.

> *What do you think is the biggest problem facing agriculture in Nagaland?*

Our inability to produce for the market is the biggest problem. It is quite ironic in that on the one hand we have the need of the populace to diversify consumption for their nutritional needs and move beyond rice, and on the other we have fruits and vegetables which are too costly even for the upper class in the society. From farm to plate, there is a missing link. The farms are too small and the entrepreneurs who can organise farmers to produce affordably for the consumers and at the same time make it profitable for the farmers do not exist.

> *Majority of farmers in Nagaland are subsistence farmers, farmers who do not produce for the market but rather for self-consumption. What measures would you take to help them?*

The National Food Security Act, 2013 in many ways have freed the farmers to go for commercial agriculture rather than being worried about sustenance. However, for that to happen, access to steady market and farmers organising themselves better would go a long way. Strengthening SHGs related to farming through cheap credit and access to market are the needs of the hour. It goes without saying that rice provided under NFSA should also be suitable for human consumption.

What is the importance of agriculture sector in an economy?

The most important contribution of agriculture to an economy is of course providing food for the common populace. This is important for providing nutritional security. Stability in food prices is needed for a stable economy. Agriculture also provides employment as well as provide raw materials to the industries.

What is organic agriculture? Is it feasible in Nagaland?

Organic agriculture is a farming system that emphasizes the use of natural processes and materials to enhance soil fertility, control pests, and promote sustainable farming practices. It avoids or largely excludes the use of synthetic chemicals, such as pesticides, fertilizers, and genetically modified organisms (GMOs). Instead, organic farming relies on techniques like crop rotation, green manure, composting, biological pest control, and the use of organic fertilizers.

The vision of an organic Nagaland has been expressed without careful study. It is true that lopsided agricultural subsidies in the country have resulted in over-application of certain fertilisers. However, that is not to say that we do not need fertilisers. More than creating a brand of organic farming, productive farming should be the vision. If organic agriculture could be produced at scale, that could be encouraged but that is not feasible at present.

What is the impact of climate change on agriculture in Nagaland?

Even without climate change, Naga farmers were struggling. With climate change, the erratic rainfall has caused much uncertainty to the farmers with many marginal farmers unable to adapt. Climate change has also resulted in growth of certain pest plants and animals not seen before.

Should we encourage National Mission on Oil Seeds and Oil Palm (NMOOP) in Nagaland?

One of the main criticisms of NMOOP is the resultant monoculture, environmental degradation and loss of water that follows. Nagaland is blessed with diverse forests and rich water resources. NMOOP will result in supply chain integrations and development of infrastructure. Farmers income will increase and standards of living will rise. The presence of landless farmers in Nagaland is minimal and thus farmers will be helped immensely. NMOOP could be introduced on pilot basis and implemented where feasible.

17

Tribalism

How would you answer?

Why does tribalism exist in Nagaland?

Why does tribalism decreases greatly once a person goes outside Nagaland?

What measures will you suggest to overcome tribalism?

Discussion

Nagaland is a tribal society. Being identified with a tribe is another layer with which an individual recognises himself or herself with – the others being clan, village and Naga as a whole. An individual's identification with a tribe has been a more recent development among the Nagas. At a time when there were no motor-able roads, and no written and spoken means of communication, tribe-consciousness was minimum. A person's identity was primarily located to his or her village. Even the Naga polity revolved around the village. We thus have "village republics" rather than "tribal chieftains" or "tribal kingdoms."

Tribe-consciousness among the Nagas began to emerge more distinctly after the British administration imposed formal categorization, which reinforced a sense of identity based on tribal affiliations. This shift was intensified by the activities of missionaries who further shaped community consciousness through their educational and religious influence[36]. Over time, this newfound tribe-consciousness became a source of tension during the Naga struggle for self-determination, contributing to factionalism, suspicion, and competition among leaders.

How certain tribes were formed deliberately in Nagaland

Among the Nagas, the formation of tribes has sometimes involved deliberate efforts to create new identities, as seen in the case of the Chakhesang tribe. Established in 1946, the Chakhesang tribe emerged from what was earlier referred to as the "Eastern Angamis" and unified the Chokri, Khezha, and Sangtam (now Pochury) groups. This conscious effort was largely driven by educated leaders from these communities, who sought to establish a collective identity distinct from other tribes.

This approach contrasts with the formation of tribes in other regions, such as parts of Africa, where tribal identities are often considered to have developed more organically over time, shaped by factors like geography, kinship systems, and socio-political changes. For example, in some African contexts, tribal boundaries were influenced by colonial interventions or historical migration patterns rather than deliberate organizational efforts.

---

[36] Jelle J. P. Wouters, "Genealogies of Nagaland's 'Tribal Democracy'," Economic & Political Weekly, June 16, 2018, https://www.epw.in/journal/2018/24/perspectives/genealogies-nagalands-tribal-democracy.html.

Similarly, other Naga tribes have also adapted and redefined their identities in response to cultural, political, or social needs, reflecting the dynamic nature of tribal affiliations in the region. While the Chakhesang case is a notable example, it illustrates broader patterns of cultural self-determination and adaptation among the Nagas.

Assertion of tribal identities as a bargaining tool

An average Naga seeks refuge under tribal identities. Since the state is not impartial, people need the security provided by the community in the form of tribes to not be discriminated against in resource sharing in areas such as government jobs, contracts, and funds. Assertion of tribal identities thus serve as a bargaining tool.

As discussed in another chapter, tribal apex bodies also serve as a protection from being bullied by Naga political groups. For a tribal apex body to threaten non-cooperation with a Naga political group is quite powerful. The irony is that both in political theory and practice, individual rights exist to protect a person against the tyranny of the state since the state in comparison to an individual is much more powerful. The Fundamental Rights in Part III of Indian Constitution also protects an individual from the state, while the issue of citizens' dealing with each other is governed by ordinary law. In Nagaland, forget about the tyranny of the state, a person can even lock up a government institution without repercussion or encroach on government land with impunity!

Usually, the manifestation of the divisiveness of tribalism is less when Nagas reside outside Nagaland in major cities in the country. However, even then, when enough Nagas from a tribe reside, tribal organisations begin to emerge. This also reveals the primacy of an individual's association with his tribal identity.

Solution to tribalism: The following could be explored as solutions to tribalism in Nagaland:

1. Cosmopolitan upbringing
2. Education
3. Kinship ties through marriage
4. Celebration of each others' cultural activities such as festivals, cloths, language and cuisine.

However, as long as tribal organisations and identities serve as bulwark against state's incompetence and inefficiencies, assertion of tribal identities will remain.

Model Answers

Why does tribalism exist in Nagaland?
Tribalism exists as a way to safeguard the community's interests. It also exists as an expression of a fear of the other.

Why does tribalism decreases greatly once a person goes outside Nagaland?

Outside Nagaland, what distinguishes a person is not the tribe but the fact that he or she is a Naga. The competitiveness associated with tribal identities reduces to a large extent.

What measures will you suggest to overcome tribalism?

Economic equality since competitive tribalism emerge from comparison. Education of each others' culture, festivals and way of life. Promotion of pan-Naga identity will go a long way towards reducing tribalism.

18

Traffic Jams in Dimapur and Kohima

How would you answer?

What are the main causes of traffic jams in Kohima?

What remedies would you suggest solving traffic jams in Nagaland?

It is obvious that increase in standard of living, increased affordability of cars, increased urbanisation, narrow roads and lack of public transportation has caused traffic jams. Why couldn't we plan ahead? What is the fundamental issue here?

Discussion

Traffic jams in Dimapur and Kohima have crossed the tipping point years ago.

Reasons for Traffic Jams

Increased Living Standards and Affordable Cars: The rise in living standards and access to more affordable cars have led to an increase in vehicle ownership. However, this growth has not been matched by adequate infrastructure planning and execution, exacerbating traffic issues.

Lack of Government Planning: A key issue is the lack of proactive planning by the government. The rapid urbanization in Kohima and Dimapur has not been accompanied by effective traffic management strategies. The absence of forward-thinking infrastructure planning has resulted in inefficient traffic flow and congestion.

Urbanisation and Zoning Laws: Haphazard urbanization and the lack of zoning laws have led to poorly planned cities, further complicating traffic management. Proper zoning and urban planning are essential for accommodating growth and reducing congestion.

Lack of Public Transport: The insufficient public transport options in Dimapur and Kohima force more people to rely on private vehicles, increasing traffic congestion. Improving and expanding public transport could alleviate some of these issues.

Impact of Traffic Jams

Loss of Productive Hours: Traffic jams significantly contribute to the loss of productive hours for individuals and businesses alike. When vehicles are stuck in congestion, commuters spend valuable time that could otherwise be used for work, leisure, or personal activities. This delay not only affects individual productivity but also has a broader economic impact, as businesses face reduced efficiency and increased operational costs. Ultimately, the cumulative effect of lost hours in traffic can hinder economic growth and diminish overall quality of life in urban areas.

Pollution and Mental Health: Traffic jams contribute significantly to air pollution, with increased vehicle emissions leading to environmental and health concerns. Additionally, the frustration of sitting in traffic can take a toll on mental health, contributing to stress and reduced overall well-being.

Parking Issues: Parking vehicles on roadsides contributes to traffic jams by narrowing available road space and creating obstacles. This issue is exacerbated by the lack of sufficient designated parking areas.

Solutions and Recommendations

Multi-Parking Schemes: Implementing multi-parking schemes can help address the shortage of parking space and reduce roadside parking.

Encouraging Public Transport: Promoting the use of public transport through improved services and incentives can decrease reliance on private vehicles.

Discouraging Private Transport: Implementing higher vehicle registration taxes could discourage excessive vehicle ownership, reducing traffic congestion. For a comparison, the road tax in Nagaland for new four-wheelers registration is 5% of the cost of the vehicle while for states like Telangana and Karnataka it ranges from 13% to 18%. Since traffic jam is mostly limited to Kohima and Dimapur, imposing high road tax throughout the state might not be feasible. At the same time, raising the road tax only for Kohima and Dimapur will lead to vehicles purchased in the two districts being registered in other districts.

Compulsory Garage Ownership: Enforcing stricter regulations for compulsory garage ownership can ensure that vehicle owners have designated parking spaces, reducing roadside parking and easing traffic flow.

Addressing these issues requires a comprehensive approach involving better urban planning, enhanced public transport options, and effective traffic management strategies to improve the overall traffic situation in Dimapur and Kohima.

Essential Insight 18.1 Singapore Model of Car Ownership

Singapore's vehicle ownership model is designed to manage traffic congestion and control the number of cars due to its limited land and high population density. To own a car, individuals must bid for a limited number of Certificates of Entitlement (COEs), which are valid for 10 years, making car ownership expensive. The city also uses an Electronic Road Pricing (ERP) system, where drivers are automatically charged for using congested roads during peak hours. These measures, along with high taxes, are used to prevent overcrowding, reduce pollution, and encourage the use of public transport, ensuring sustainable urban mobility. It goes without saying that Singapore has one of the best public transport systems in the world.

MODEL ANSWERS

What are the main causes of traffic jams in Kohima?

Increased disposable income and affordable vehicles, lack of proper zoning laws, lack of urban planning and lack of public transport are some reasons for traffic jams in Kohima and Dimapur.

What remedies would you suggest solving traffic jams in Nagaland?

Encouraging public transport and discouraging private vehicle ownership by providing both incentives and disincentives, enforcing traffic rules, developing multi parking schemes and developing urban infrastructure are some ways to mitigate urban congestion. It is obvious that increase in standard of living, increased affordability of cars, increased urbanisation, narrow roads and lack of public transportation has caused traffic jams.

Why couldn't we plan ahead? What is the fundamental issue here?

 In the Indian constitutional scheme, it is well known that the central government has a disproportionate share of power. Since Nagaland does not generate own revenue, the dependence of the state government on the central government is more. This has resulted in a phenomenon where Nagaland in many ways is merely a spoke in the wheel implementing the visions of the central government. Widening roads and constructing flyovers in urban areas will take significant resources which the state on its own cannot afford. Secondly, our institutions also need to develop courage. We have a system where everything is personalised. Our urban centers are becoming cosmopolitan but the people holding the positions are still viewed through the lens of the community. Laws have to be passed and the laws implemented impartially without fear or favour on issues such as urban land encroachment.

19

Professionalism in Government Service: Need of the Hour

How would you answer?

Often people complain about the non-functioning of government institution in Nagaland due to reasons such as employees' absence, employees coming to work intoxicated or the files simply being left to pile up. This can be characterised as lack of professionalism. Why do you think this problem exist in government institutions/offices in Nagaland?

Discussion

Fixed working hours where employees come to the workplace on time in the morning and leave at set time in the evening are a result of the Industrial Revolution. This period saw the rise of factories and mass production, which necessitated a structured and consistent work schedule to ensure efficiency and productivity. The standardisation of working hours was further solidified by labor movements advocating for fair working conditions and the introduction of labor laws.

Lack of professionalism in government service is one of the biggest issues facing Naga society. The symptoms of lack of professionalism can be highlighted as given below:

1.   **Lack of regular attendance at workplace.** This problem is worse in remote areas. An officer whose signature is mandatory for applying certain schemes could be absent for months at a time giving undue hardship to the people. That this problem is worse in remote areas where the beneficiary could be illiterate and poor with no means of travel makes this problem more severe. Even when the employee-concerned is present at the workplace, he or she might not be available throughout the day, present only for an hour or two.

2.   **Coming to the workplace intoxicated.** This is also an issue people have complains but are powerless to do anything about.

3.   **Improper handling of files.** The employees fail to show up at their workplace and the files are sent to their place of residence to get their signatures.

4. **Non-compliance with administrative protocols.** The government, for efficiency and sensitivities, establishes administrative protocols. For reporting crime, certain protocols are put in place to protect the privacy of the victims as well as help the law enforcement in investigation and prosecution. For health and safety of the public, protocols are established for hotels, restaurants and eateries with the public health department tasked to check them from time to time. For secret and sensitive information, file confidentiality has to be maintained. In all these cases, the protocols

set are not followed leading to victimisation and trauma, health risks being ignored and confidential information being leaked out.

Origins of the problem:

Nagas were not accustomed to fixed office working hours. The government with all its administrative machinery and protocols were new to Nagas. Not only that, initially, people did not forego their life of farming even after working in government sector. Working in government service was to earn money whereas working as a farmer served the role of producing food. Growing up in rural areas, one hears older generations give advice "Even directors, once they retire, have to take up farming." There are even stories about how headmasters of schools made their students work in their personal fields or fields belonging to the school. The famous statement made by a Naga pioneer, A Kevichusa, "I am a farmer like my ancestors before me: trying to make two plates of rice grow where only one grew before" captured the Naga mindset succinctly. Pride is associated with farming.

The government employee to population ratio in Nagaland is very high. This has led to a scenario where works could be piled up and resolved at convenient hours. Office works with daily deadlines are limited only to certain offices.

Government jobs are very secure. One hardly ever hears of a government employee been dismissed from work on account of non-performance, absence or non-professional behaviour.

Promotion in government service mostly depends on seniority rather than performance. This also affects the motivation and performance of government employees.

Nagas' penchant for holding different programs: Government employees serve as important staffers to different programs. Even high-ranking government employees are found actively involved in different cultural and religious activities. Many departments have office Christmas programs! No where in the world will one find such enthusiastic participation from government employees in such extra curricular activities outside of their active workplace. An acquaintance of this author once lamented: "We went to collect data from X office. We were greeted with the response: 'The director and his colleagues are practising songs for Christmas. Please come another time.'"

Lack of professional behaviour at the workplace is not unique to Nagaland. The problem arises where the concept of fixed working hours throughout the year is not instilled in the minds of the people. A recent news report in the Print[37] narrates how Industries in Tamil Nadu are facing problems because workers from Bihar and Uttar Pradesh leaves whenever they want during festivals. Instilling in them the need to respect the sanctity of contract and labour laws have been an uphill battle.

It takes time and effort to develop professionalism in the workplace. It will take both reforms from the top and pressure from below to change the current lack of professionalism in the workplace. An enlightened civil society that pressurises the government to deliver will go a long way in promoting professionalism in the workplace.

---

[37]Sagrika Kissu, "In Tamil Nadu's Tiruppur, Bihari migrants are the new business bosses. Who do they employ?" *The Print,* March 6, 2024, https://theprint.in/ground-reports/in-tamil-nadus-tiruppur-bihari-migrants-are-the-new-business-bosses-who-do-they-employ/1989935/

Often people complain about the non-functioning of government institution in Nagaland due to reasons such as employees' absence, employees coming to work intoxicated or the files simply being left to pile up. This can be characterised as lack of professionalism. Why do you think this problem exist in government institutions/offices in Nagaland?

The incentive structure in government services is flawed. A person is rarely dismissed for non-performance or dereliction of duty. A person's pay or promotion does not depend on performance but rather on seniority. All these are meant to protect the employees so that they can perform without fear of losing their jobs. However, these lead to non-professionalism. Added to these is the excess employees in government service. Often, the existence of disguised unemployment in agriculture is discussed but it could be worst in government sector. A person's professionalism in Nagaland emerges from their work ethics rather than from the professionalism of institutions, which is still undergoing development

20

Interview Suggestions

Congratulations for making this far! You are ahead of 95% of aspirants for making till the interview stage. You are now at a very crucial point of the exam process! The 30 minutes in the interview is high-risk, high-reward opportunity. Remember the most important point: interview is a conversation. You will find that it is more like a discussion where you exchange views. Some NPSC exam veterans go to chat with NPSC chairman!

An interview, in the context of competitive exams in Nagaland, have three layers:

I.	Personal

II.	Issues related to Nagaland

III.	Current Affairs

I.	Personal

A) Your studies

B) Your work

C) Your village

D) Your tribe and district

A) Your studies

- The institutions you attended – schooling and higher education
- Your favourite subject
- A question from your favourite subject

- Why you like the subject
- The toughest paper
- Why you failed a certain paper (do not narrate long stories here!)
- Any concept from your area of expertise can be expected.

B) Your current work

- Suggestions on how you could improve your workplace (do not criticise your co-workers, including your boss)
- Your contributions or the nature of your work
- A recent project or work you carried out
- Problems your workplace is facing
- How your work experience can be used to contribute to the job you are applying
- Why you prefer the new job you are applying

C) Your village
- Meaning of your village's name
- Important personalities from your village
- Important schemes or projects taking place in your village at present
- Your leaders - who is your VDB secretary, VC chairman, VEC chairman, Students' Union president etc.
- Tourist places, historical places or any peculiar or famous special practice in your village
- No. of clans and khels
- Institutions in your village such as Primary Health Centre, Government Middle School – their contributions and problems they are facing

D) Your tribe/district
- Important personalities
- Tourist places or historical places in your district
- Any peculiar or famous special practice from your tribe. For example, Ahngs for Konyaks, War Dance for Semas, Wrestling for Chakhesangs and Angamis etc.
- Institutions in your district: No. Of colleges, higher secondary schools, ADC, EAC, who is present DC, etc.
- Constituencies and MLAs
- Your tribe material and non-material culture and their significance, including festivals, cloths, games, and practices

II.   Issues related to Nagaland
- Issues facing Nagaland: The present book seeks to help aspirants in this area. Model questions in the book are very specific. You can expect questions to be more general such as "What is your view on FMR?" Or "What is your view on ILP?" When the question is very specific, eg. "Should ILP be implemented in Dimapur?" Give a brief answer about ILP, then show your understanding of the issue by contrasting Dimapur with other districts.
- Significance of Naga cultural practices: feast of merit, yoddling, house horns, etc.

III.   Current Affairs
A) World
B) India
C) Nagaland

- Unlike your prelims where you have to prepare current affairs of events upto a year, for your interview, the current affairs is mostly of a few months or a few weeks.
- Pay attention to the names, places and the issues

On the day of interview

- Dress properly
- Sit straight
- Look at the interviewers in the eye
- Project confidence
- Project authority: in the course of mock interviews, we come across many aspirants who say they want to be in uniform service as DSP but slunk in the chair and refuse to look at the interviewers in the eyes.
- When introducing yourself, do not make it too long
- Talk to them as equals. Once you clear the exam, who knows, you might even be working in the same office
- Don't get cocky. Eventually, they are the ones who will give you marks
- Don't preach!
- It is alright to disagree with the interviewers as long as your disagreements are valid but if the interviewer is an expert or your facts are wrong, being stubborn and sticking to your point will leave a bad impression
- Don't let the interviewers do all the talking. It can happen that you agree with the interviewer on every point, and you have no more points to add. In such instances, there is always the danger of the candidate saying "Yes" and "I agree" to everything the interviewer says with the candidate speaking very little. Having said next to nothing, the interviewers have no content in their hands to assess. In such instances, you

can always bring points which are relevant to the discussion - a side point or even a criticism which exists even though you agree with the interviewers. "Sir, what you said is right but there is the other point to consider" or "Sir, I agree with you. On this, I recently read about something which I feel is relevant"

- The interviewers could test you by demeaning you or your community or your work, walk around, tear papers, or pick up the phone. Do not lose your composure.

- As far as possible, do not criticise the government. If asked about challenges or shortcomings in governance, frame your response positively. For example, instead of saying, "The government has failed in XYZ," you could say, "There is room for improvement in XYZ, and these steps could enhance effectiveness."

- You will be a government employee, not an activist. Be realistic. You are being assessed for your ability to work within the system and contribute constructively, not as an activist or critic.

- You can ask a few seconds to frame your answer

- Take a second or two before answering. Blurting out the answer as soon as the question is finished conveys insincerity

- You can request permission to attempt an answer even though you are not sure

- If the interviewer asks a difficult question of which you know the answer but you need to organise your thoughts and you do not want to take more time thinking or the pause is already quite long, a trick is to frame your answer by repeating the question. This will also clarify the question in your mind

Preparing for your interview

- The newspaper the Morung Express carry many analytical works on issues facing Nagaland
- Explained pages on Indian express and the Hindu newspapers
- Observing the society
- Talking to elders. Put yourselves in their shoes and find where they are coming
- Practising in front of mirror

21

Facing the Panel – My Interview Experience

a) NPSC CESE – 2022

Interview Transcript – Common Education Service (Economics)

Dated: 30/05/2023

Candidate: Please, may I come in?

Interviewers: Come in.

NPSC Chairman: Come over here, show your documents. You may take your seat.

Candidate: Thank you, Sir.

NPSC Chairman: Okay, get started.

Candidate: My name is Chothazo Nienu. I am from Thenyizumi Village, from Phek district. And I am a Chakhesang. I am pursuing a PhD from the University of Hyderabad; at the same time, I am preparing for competitive exams. The topic of my thesis is Community Participation in Education and Communitisation of Elementary Education in Nagaland.

NPSC Chairman: Mr. Nienu, you're pursuing a PhD, you have come for the interview to teach graduate students, and your research is on elementary education. What is the point of your research? I don't see a reason as to why you should focus on elementary education.

Candidate: Sir, as you know, human capital is a big part of Economics. Under human capital, education plays a prominent role. Within education, one cannot ignore elementary education.

NPSC Chairman: Our society is in a dark place. Nagas seems to have no sense of progress. Why do you think this is happening?

Candidate: Sir, I agree that when we look around, we see a lot of problems. However, I believe that it is also important that we look back and reflect on where we have come from. Just 70–80 years ago, it is said that there were certain corners even in Nagaland which were practicing head-hunting. We have come a long way. As a society, we want to progress quickly, but we need to realise there will be growth pains. If we reflect on where we actually started and see how far we have come, I think there is room for optimism.

NPSC Chairman: Okay, your thesis is on Communitisation. Do you think we should scrap this policy? In your thesis, what are some recommendations on Communitisation based on what you have studied?

Candidate: Sir, as you know, Communitisation is an institutional innovation. Many states across the country have adopted certain features of Communitisation. The School Management Committees, the Village Education Committees, which focus on decentralisation, are features of Communitisation others have borrowed[38]. We should

---

[38] Upon later reflection, I would like to clarify that while Nagaland's Communitisation policy was innovative, institutional features like School Management Committees (SMCs) and Village Education Committees (VECs) had already been introduced under national programs such as the Sarva Shiksha Abhiyan and later formalized in the Right to Education Act, 2009.

not think about scrapping this policy. However, we need to go back to the basics and find out why Communitisation has worked wonderfully in certain villages and has not worked in others.

(NPSC Chairman interrupts to add: In some cases, they have become worse.)

Candidate continues: I did my fieldwork in Kohima district and Mon district. We need to find out why they have worked wonderfully in villages like Jakhama and Viswema, where I carried out my fieldwork, and find out why they have not worked in other places. The state government has to conduct studies, compare and contrast, and find the reasons. When Communitisation was first introduced, there was a lot of enthusiasm, and it worked wonderfully. We need to assess what we have done right and what we have done wrong.

NPSC Chairman: I would recommend you to include your recommendations and present your thesis to the Chief Secretary and Education Secretary once you finish your thesis. Anyway, the New Education Policy has been introduced. There are many wonderful features from the new policy which villagers will not be able to follow. The NEP is too complicated. What will happen to Communitisation now that the NEP is being introduced?

Candidate: Sir, one feature of Communitisation is participation. The other is training. Training the villagers is inherent within Communitisation. The government has to think about following its commitments to what it has passed in the Act.

These were not directly borrowed from Nagaland, though there may be similarities in decentralization objectives.

Second Interviewer: I want you to agree or disagree with the statement: "Educated people are the reason for the problems in the state."

Candidate: Sir, can you please elaborate on the term "problems in the state" and what you mean by it?

Second Interviewer: If we look at any social disharmony, it is educated people who are often at the forefront in these situations. It seems they are the ones causing problems. Would you agree or disagree and elaborate that educated Nagas are the problems in the society?

Candidate: Sir, there is no doubt that when a person is truly educated, education is an asset to himself and the society. However, on your statement. In my place, a Chief Guest at the Students' Union program once compared people who are not properly educated to *'Cekho'* in my dialect. If you go to a traditional Naga kitchen, there's the fireplace and on top, the ceiling where we keep items such as baskets and other household items. In between, there is an item called *'Cekho'* where we keep items like akhuni, chilis, etc. The *Cekho* is neither up nor down. *(The interview members laughed at this comparison.)* When a person is truly educated, he goes on to achieve big things for himself and the society. On the other hand, a person who is graduated and is unemployed refuses to do menial work such as driving, farming, etc. He would gladly take up a peon work if it was a govt job, but if it wasn't, he refuses to be gainfully employed. Frustrated and with a sense of importance, at the slightest provocation, he writes angrily on social media and leads others to protest sites. While it is unfortunate, one has to agree in many ways that educated people are the reason for problems in the state.

Third Interviewer (a woman): You mentioned *Cekho.* Mention the things which are found there.

Candidate: In a *Cekho,* we find akhuni, chili for drying, spoons while cooking. *(NPSC Chairman interrupts: Plates also at times?*

Candidate: Yes, even plates.

Third Interviewer: That means *Cekho* is useful!

Candidate: Madam, I only took *Cekho* as a picture to drive a point on people who are not properly educated. I am not undermining *Cekho* in any way.

(NPSC members laugh again)

Third Interviewer: You mention the educated people's wrong attitude to menial work. Who do you think is responsible for the attitude? Is it society, education system, teachers, students?

Candidate: I think ultimately, it is the society. While we do not want to admit it, it comes out unconsciously in our conversations: "He has graduated but he is working only as a driver." This attitude has to change.

Third Interviewer: Do you have experience of teaching?

Candidate: While I was in the University of Hyderabad, there were often group discussions. I have also presented papers and taken part in department presentations.

Third Interviewer: But you do not have classroom teaching experience?

Candidate: No, Ma'am, I do not.

Third Interviewer: And you want to pursue a career in it?

Candidate: Yes, Ma'am.

Third Interviewer: Do you think Communitisation was entirely original or it was rooted in our history?

Candidate: Madam, it can be said that *Morungs* served as the precursor to Communitisation. *Morungs* were places where young people would come to socialise and learn. The community had a stake in their education, and this idea has been transferred to Communitisation.

Third Interviewer: Fine, I am done.

NPSC Chairman to Third Interviewer: You are done? Next one then.

(Candidate tries to leave)

NPSC Chairman: Not yet.

Fourth Interviewer: I often observe hopelessness among our young population. Why do you think this has happened in the state?

Candidate: Sir, in Economics, there is a concept called the Dutch Disease. In the Netherlands, when oil and natural gas were discovered, it led to an imbalance in the development of the country. The oil and gas sector developed while the other sectors were ignored. The problem was exacerbated by the strengthening of the Dutch currency. I believe we have our own version of the Dutch Disease. The government sector is well developed while the private sector is not. To get a government job, which is not very tough, means your future is fairly guaranteed with good pay and pensions. This has led to a situation where everyone wants to be a government employee. Since everyone cannot be a government employee, it has led to a situation where if a person does not get a government job, the person feels his world has crashed and has no place in society.

Fourth Interviewer: Many young Nagas have gone to join the army, and it has benefitted the youth a lot in our state. Do you think the Agniveer scheme will adversely impact them?

Candidate: The Agniveer scheme was introduced with the aim to cut costs. Modern warfare has changed with more focus on technicals and engineers. One of the impacts of the policy on Naga youth will be that there will be less recruitment. Not only that, since they will be trained in the ways of using arms, we have to be careful that those who come back are not frustrated since there is every possibility of them taking up arms because of our unresolved political issue.

Fifth Interviewer: I have gone over your mark scripts. Since you have scored well in Indian Economy, I want to ask a question on that. In India, the tertiary sector is well developed while the manufacturing sector is not. Why do you think this is the case?

Candidate: Madam, it is observed that economies often take a path where the manufacturing sector is developed before the tertiary sector. This has not happened in India because of the wage differential between foreign countries and India. The wages in India are still low compared to Western countries, while India has a huge stock of qualified low-wage workers due to emphasis on subjects like Math, Science, and Engineering. This has led to a huge amount of outsourcing into India, especially in tech services.

Fifth Interviewer: What about Nagaland? In Nagaland, the education sector has developed. Should we focus on the manufacturing sector?

Candidate: Madam, as you know, the tertiary sector in Nagaland consists not only of education but other areas such as transport and hotels which are doing quite okay. However, for Nagaland, I would recommend that we focus on organic agriculture and cash crops. Let other states focus on manufacturing in keeping with our economic theory of comparative advantage.

NPSC Chairman interrupts: About manufacturing, we can think about extracting resources from the ground.

Candidate: Sir, the problem with that model is that the moment natural resources are discovered, land ownership becomes an issue, not forgetting the threats issued by different political groups.

NPSC Chairman: But these problems cannot go on forever. These issues will always be there and we eventually have to tackle them.

Candidate: Sir, I was actually discussing this issue with a friend of mine for the interview because there are mineral resources in Meluri sub-division under Phek district. *(NPSC Chairman laughs at this point)* Even if we tackle these institutional factors, we have to admit that there are a lot of infrastructural issues to tackle. For transport of mineral resources, proper roads have to be built. For employing workers who will have children, there have to be proper schools, health centers, proper drinking water facilities, and regular electricity. There is still a long way to go.

NPSC Chairman: Okay, we are done. We had a great discussion today, right?

Candidate: Yes, Sir. It was a great experience. Thank you.

Result: Selected for the post of Assistant Professor, Economics Department, Higher Education

21

Facing the Panel – My Interview Experience

b) NPSC Technical – 2023

Candidate: Please may I come in?

NPSC Chairman: Please come in!

(The interview room was small, with a modest table placed between the candidate and three interviewers. Compared to the NPSC CESE interview, the setting felt more intimate — the candidate was seated barely three feet away from the panel. Any nervousness or hesitation would have been easily noticeable.)

The candidate handed over the documents to the NPSC Chairman.

NPSC Chairman: You may introduce yourself.

Candidate: My name is Chothazo Nienu. I cleared the recently conducted NPSC CESE exam and am currently serving as an Assistant Professor in the Department of Economics at Pfutsero Government College. I am also pursuing a PhD from the University of Hyderabad on the topic "Community Participation in Education and Communitisation of Elementary Education in Nagaland"

NPSC Chairman: Oh! You're already working as an Assistant Professor, your first preference will be Economics and Statistics Officer then?

Candidate: Yes, sir.

NPSC Chairman: I'm glad to hear you're doing research on Communitisation. I'm interested in your research. Will you share your thesis with me?

Candidate: Certainly, sir. I can find your contact details and share the soft copy with you.

NPSC Chairman: What is your opinion on Communitisation?

Candidate: Communitisation has worked wonderfully in certain villages, whereas the ground situation has remained unchanged in many others. This aligns with broader research on community participation, which shows that communities with strong leadership and organisation benefit more from such programmes, while poorly organised ones may even suffer setbacks.

NPSC Chairman: Okay. Have you heard of Amartya Sen?

Candidate: Yes, he is a famous Indian economist.

NPSC Chairman: Can you tell me when and why he won the Nobel Prize?

Candidate: I'm not completely sure, sir. I think he won it around the year 2000 for his work in Welfare Economics?

Note: Amartya Sen won the Nobel Prize in Economic Sciences in 1998 for his contributions to welfare economics, particularly in the areas of poverty, famine, and human development.

NPSC Chairman: Okay!

(The Chairman then nodded to the first panellist to continue.)

First Panellist: What are the two kinds of taxes?

Candidate: Direct taxes and indirect taxes.

First Panellist: Among indirect taxes, there are taxes imposed by the excise department on alcohol and tobacco products, right? Why are these taxes imposed?

Candidate: Sir, there are two main reasons:

1. For revenue generation. Since the price elasticity of demand for these goods is low, even high taxes don't drastically reduce consumption. As such, it is a stable source of revenue.

2. To discourage consumption. These are sin goods, and the government wants to reduce their use due to health and social costs.

First Panellist: Okay, the second point was the answer I was looking for.

Third Panellist: Since your research is on Communitisation, are there conflicts in villages between VECs and SMDCs?

(Before the candidate could respond, the NPSC Chairman interjected.)

NPSC Chairman: What are SMDCs?

Third Panellist: SMDCs are School Management and Development Committees that oversee planning, budgeting, and implementation of school improvement activities under Sarva Shiksha Abhiyan (SSA). There have been cases where they clash with the VECs.

NPSC Chairman: That's unfortunate!

Candidate: The understanding is that the VEC (Village Education Committee) oversees all schools in the village, while the SMDC is specific to individual schools. Since school development funds are credited directly to the SMDC's account, it can lead to jealousy, mistrust, and a feeling among VEC members that they have lost control.

NPSC Chairman: Okay, good. You may leave. Be sure to finish your research!

Candidate: Thank you, sir.

Result: Initially selected as Inspector of Statistics and later promoted to Economics and Statistics Officer after another candidate backed out.

www.ingramcontent.com/pod-product-compliance
Lightning Source LLC
Chambersburg PA
CBHW021527150726
47990CB00006B/2132